Grange Hill Home and Away

With Grange Hillites let loose in their walking boots in the Austrian Alps anything can happen. While Zammo and Jonah acquire a taste for apfel strudel and cable cars, Pogo pursues another local attraction – with pigtails. The arrival of a neighbouring German school party equals trouble, but even that's nothing compared to the state Gripper Stebson lands in. Meanwhile, Suzanne is taking careful note of all the carryings-on; she knows somebody back home who will be very interested to hear all the news . . .

ROBERT LEESON

Grange Hill
Home and Away

Based on the BBC television series
GRANGE HILL
by Phil Redmond

FONTANA · LIONS

First published in Fontana Lions September 1982
by William Collins Sons & Co. Ltd
14 St James's Place, London SW1

Copyright © Robert Leeson and Phil Redmond 1982

Printed in Great Britain by
William Collins Sons & Co. Ltd, Glasgow

Chapter 1

People are funny. Every year it's the same. As soon as
Christmas dinner is over, the last mince pie pulled and the
last cracker eaten, what do they do? They start thinking
about summer. Not the work bit, the exams and so forth, but
– would you believe? the holidays.

Imagine it, all over town, Grange Hillites of all ages,
shapes and sizes, stretched out at home, stuffed with turkey
and pud, all with their minds on a long, long rest, in the sun.
And not just the troops, the staff as well. Teachers are
human, too.

There was Douglas (Pogo) Patterson, hands folded over
his tum as he lay on the settee and watched a repeat of *Sound
of Music* (actually it was his mother's choice; he wanted the
James Bond film on the other channel).

Pogo had his eyes half closed anyway. He was dreaming
about more food, a long holiday in one of those stately
homes where large ladies in long skirts serve medieval
banquets, roast ox or ostrich with a six-foot plum duff to
follow.

Jonah Jones was thinking about summer, but not really
enjoying the thought. He'd been told, that day, where the
family was going. Four weeks in a self-catering cottage. Mrs
Jones was going to do the catering, not the cottage. A place
by the sea on a remote Scottish island. It wasn't just that. It
meant all the schemes he and Zammo Maguire had worked
out for the summer were knocked on the head. So he was not
his usual cheery self.

Fay Lucas had no idea where she might land up in the
summer. Somewhere hot, abroad, she hoped, where she
could wear new summer gear and meet terrific boys.
Annette Firman didn't care where she landed as long as
there was a good crowd to mess about with. She had a good

time, any time. She didn't dream about fun. She organised it.

Suzanne Ross knew where she was going. Nowhere. There wasn't the cash in the house for holidays. In fact there was only one time more boring than holidays, and that was the bit in between.

And let's not forget Stebson, Gripper Stebson. Let's be honest, though, he was not thinking about holidays. In his business, making people miserable, there are no holidays. Gripper was on duty all the time. He had plans for the coming year. But they were not relaxing ones.

Among the veterans, too, there were thoughts of summer. Alan Humphreys was running over in his mind where he and Susi MacMahon might go. This would be the first year they could get away together without their parents taking out an insurance policy – or hiring a private detective. He wasn't very clear where they would go but he had a feeling that Susi would make up their minds for them.

Tucker Jenkins, being more masterful, had his priorities worked out. This summer he was taking to the road on the Bonny his cousin had promised to lend him. It was true it was ten years old and it did tend to piddle oil a little when you pushed it over twenty-five on the motorway. But it moved. It had a good pillion seat. The only thing to be decided was who would have the honour of sitting there. Tucker had half made his mind up – Pamela Cartwright could get lucky. She didn't know yet, but she soon would.

Meanwhile, back at the ranch, Bullet Baxter put the thought of Grange Hill from him and let idle fancies run through his head, like fishing in a distant trout stream, with evenings in front of the fire holding a large glass of malt whisky.

Miss Lexington saw herself strolling through narrow streets in an Italian town, with the bright blue sky and sunshine above.

Miss Mooney and Graham Sutcliffe, having had a little tiff over Christmas dinner over where they might go next summer, were glowering at each other and wondering

6

whether they might not have to organise two holidays, not one.

What none of them knew was that somewhere else Mother Christmas had made plans for them. Their summer holidays had already been decided. They were all going to the same place. Though she hadn't worked out where, yet.

Who is Mother Christmas you ask? But read on.

Chapter 2

One evening at the start of the new term, the staff room at Grange Hill was crowded. But there was no pottering about with tea cups, or stuffing cases with papers and saying quick goodnights.

Everyone sat quietly. Only Dan Hopwood was on his feet, reading slowly from a paper he held.

'And as for salaries, talks with the authorities are due to open soon. No one sounds too hopeful. The Government is talking about a four per cent increase and no more.'

'Except for police and High Court Judges,' interrupted McGuffey who sat, feet up, at the back of the room, among the younger teachers.

Hopwood raised his eyebrows and went on with his reading.

'Our employers have said nothing yet. But the word is going round that they will offer three per cent.'

'What per cent?' demanded Baxter. There was a buzz of conversation. Hopwood lifted his hand.

'They say the ratepayers will not stand for any more on the wages bill.'

'But that will leave us worse off than last year,' said Miss Lexington.

'Indeed,' returned Baxter, 'even I without your mathematical expertise, can work that out. We can't take that lying down . . .'

Hopwood pressed on: 'We cannot really decide what to do until we definitely know what they are offering us. But we should work out what we are prepared to do.'

McGuffey jumped up: 'I think we ought to pull the plug out . . .'

'Call a spade a spade,' shouted someone. 'Do you mean strike?'

'I do mean strike. All the messing about does nothing. Letters to the Council, meetings, lobbies. Proper action is what we need. They take notice of people like ASLEF.'

'We're teaching children, not driving trains,' said Miss Mooney excitedly. 'We have to think of them, and their parents.'

'Hm,' muttered Baxter. 'I wish the parents would think about us for a change.' He raised his fingers and counted off.

'Last week, two parents' meetings. I came to school at 8.30 in the morning, and I left at 10 o'clock in the evening. Saturday afternoon, two teams in the district cup to supervise. Home about six.'

He paused: 'That's what? six, twelve, sixteen hours overtime. And unpaid. Which among the public would put up with that?'

'Ah, but they say we get longer holidays.'

'Yes, and spend half of 'em marking, working out time tables, etc.'

Dan Hopwood listened to the growing row and wondered for the twentieth time that term how he had landed himself in this job as teachers' representative. The truth was, there had been no big rush for the position, but everyone else had decided he would do nicely. So he had to soldier on for the rest of the year. He banged on the table.

'Let's have a bit of hush. There's some doubt about whether teachers up and down the country are ready to shut the schools down.'

'Hear hear,' called Miss Mooney.

'But a lot of people think there is a case for a withdrawal of goodwill.'

'What goodwill?' demanded someone.

Dan Hopwood smiled. 'Do you mind? It has been suggested we might, as a protest, refuse to carry out activities over and above the call of duty.'

'Such as?'

'Such as evening meetings with the public. Weekend activities. Lunchtime duties.'

9

'Lunchtime?'

'Right. We must be the only profession in the country that works during its lunch hour.'

'We couldn't pull out at lunch time,' said Miss Mooney. 'There'd be chaos.'

'Good thing too,' called McGuffey. 'Then they'd realise they're getting teachers on the cheap.'

'Teachers?' said Sutcliffe. 'Childminders, you mean.'

He and Miss Mooney turned and glared at one another. Hopwood cleared his throat.

'I think we should bring this meeting to a close in the formal sense. By our next meeting we should know where we stand.'

The meeting broke up and groups of teachers headed for the door.

At that moment, in came Mr Keating. He apologised to Hopwood.

'Sorry I couldn't make it. But the Governors' meeting dragged on. Did I miss much?'

Hopwood smiled. 'You missed a lively argument about all the things we should stop doing in our spare time to make the public sit up and take notice.'

'Oh.' Keating's face fell.

'What have your mob been talking about?' demanded Baxter.

Keating paused. 'I shall report to staff at the coffee break tomorrow.' But he went on: 'I can reveal one thing. Grange Hill is to have its first school journey abroad for four years.'

'Thanks for telling us. Whose brilliant idea is this?'

Keating's eyebrows rose.

'The Head's.' He hesitated. 'Now I come to think about it, it did seem a bit on the spur of the moment.'

'Oh yes?' Groups of teachers drew in closer.

'Yes, one of the governors was making a little speech about the need not to drive the children too hard, all work and no play, and so on. Then the head said, "Yes, the time has come for an easing in the routine and one thought is a trip abroad, something to tie in with geography and foreign languages. But to be a treat, especially for the younger pupils".'

'She might have thought that up on the spur of the moment,' put in Sutcliffe. 'But now someone else will have to do the work.'

Keating smiled: 'I believe a list of possible people is being drawn up. She may be seeing them tomorrow. She never wastes time.'

'Just let me guess who's on the list?'

'Tut tut, Graham,' said Baxter. 'What you need now is some light refreshment. Who's for the King's Arms?'

'Right behind you, Geoff. You're paying, of course.'

'I was rather hoping someone else might, in return for my account of the last Grange Hill school journey abroad.'

'That'll be a change from your stories about school camp.'

'Well, let's get this show on the road,' called Baxter.

The staff room emptied and the teachers streamed down the corridors and out into the dark evening air.

Chapter 3

'You need four things to make a success of a school journey abroad.'

Baxter, comfortably seated next to the fire in the bar at the King's Arms, raised his glass and saluted the half dozen teachers who sat around him.

'And they are?' said Hopwood.

'It should not be too far away to wear you out before you get there. It should not be too near in case some of 'em start wanting to go home again after the first two days. It should be cheap and easy, no visas, no vaccinations. It should be energetic without being dangerous. It should not be too far away from civilisation, not too close to large towns where kids can get lost and cause mayhem.'

'That's seven things at least,' said Miss Lexington. 'Your maths are shaky, Geoff.'

'How about an educational cruise? The crew look after them. You sit in the sun all day and the bar all evening.'

'No, too expensive. £300 a time and you find yourself stuck up a creek with a bent propellor and spending your days in the local fossil museum.'

'How about a ski-ing holiday?'

'Too late, even for spring ski-ing. The boss is a bit behind-hand with her brilliant idea.'

'How about one of those safari adventure trips, like down the Nile in a felucca.'

'A what?'

'I saw there was one trip to China, less than £200 apiece.'

'Pull the other one, old son. You've been reading those lying articles in educational journals.'

Baxter drank deeply.

'No, I expect we'll land up with a ten day trip to Luxemburg on a coach.'

'Trouble with coach trips is you spend too much time on the road. The kids barely get the chance to settle down. Go by air and you don't lose more than a day.'

'Air costs too much.'

'You can charter.'

'What? A Tiger Moth? Be realistic. We'll be talking about fifty pupils maximum, about six or seven staff and about £150 a throw.'

'£150?' asked McGuffey. That'll put it out of the reach of a good few kids.'

'Let's ease up a bit,' put in Hopwood. 'Every time I relax with a bunch of teachers it turns into a meeting.'

'Quite right,' said Baxter. 'Who's having another?'

'Not me, I'm driving. Anyway, it's getting late. I think I'll head for home.'

The group finished their drinks and moved slowly across the pub lounge and out through the swing door. As they left Miss Lexington turned to Miss Mooney.

'Terri, did you notice those two young ladies at the table in the far corner?'

Miss Mooney half turned: 'Goodness me, I missed them. But I doubt I would have recognised them – out of uniform. They change overnight when they leave school, don't they.'

As the last of the teachers left, the two girls at the table turned to one another and burst out laughing.

'Did you see that, Susi?' said Pamela Cartwright. 'The whole lot of them marched past us and didn't say a word.'

'They've probably forgotten us already,' chuckled Susi MacMahon. 'After all, that's life. One moment you're there, next moment you're off the register.'

'Changing the subject,' said Pamela, 'made your mind up what you're doing this summer? Do you feel like teaming up with someone?'

Susi frowned. 'Don't know. Wish you'd asked me earlier. I've more or less fixed up to go with Alan.'

'Yes, they are a bit of a pain, aren't they?'

'Who do you mean, they?'

'Well, I had Peter on the phone the other night. Offering me the chance of riding pillion on some oily machine of his, out in the wilds. He seemed to think it was some kind of honour.'

'What did you say?'

'I burst out laughing.'

'You didn't. What did he say to that?'

'He didn't say anything.'

'Was he offended?'

'Might have been. But Mr Jenkins shouldn't think I come running when he nods his head. Pity you're fixed up with Alan though. I'll have to think of something else.'

Chapter 4

How it happened, no one knew, but the following morning the news was all around the school. Everybody knew there was going to be a school trip abroad. Everybody knew how much it would cost and everybody knew where they were going. The one problem was, everybody had different information.

'It's a cruise down the Rhine,' announced someone as 2N crowded into their classroom.

'Never,' said Zammo Maguire, 'a barge trip up the Regent's Canal more likely.'

'Well, it's abroad, that's for sure.'

'Right,' put in a new arrival. 'The school's taking a farmhouse in the North of France.'

'Great – milking cows and mucking out stables.'

'Oh no, horse riding and sailing. My cousin went on one last year.'

'Sailing – on a farm? Don't be stupid.'

'It could be one of those working holiday holidays you know grape picking, or chopping trees down, or herding reindeer or skin-diving.'

'Stop it, I'm getting over-excited.'

'I wouldn't mind. Better than sitting in a streaming wet tent eating cold sausage and doing a wild life project.'

'I saw this leaflet in the library. They do some fantastic things – elephant riding in India, and crocodile spotting in Peru.'

'Who holds the crocodiles still?'

'What are you raving about?'

'I mean, while you put the spots on.'

'I'm laughing myself silly.'

The classroom was nearly full as Miss Mooney rushed in. She looked grim.

'Hey miss, where are we going?'

'Going? You're not going anywhere.'

'On the school journey, miss.'

She stared: 'How do you all know about that? It hasn't even been decided yet.'

'Ah,' said Annette. 'We make it our business to know what's going on.'

'No doubt you do, Annette. But at the moment you know more than me. No doubt there will be more information shortly, in which case, I'll let you know – or you'll let me.'

She dived into her bag: 'Now, if you'll quieten down, I'll hand out these forms about medicals for you to take home for your parents.'

As Miss Mooney rummaged among her papers, Jonah suddenly turned to Zammo.

'Hey, that's it. We're going.'

'What d'you mean?'

'On the trip.'

'I don't want to go on any trip.'

'Yes you do.'

'Why?'

'Think, man. If we both go on the school trip, I don't have to stay in that shack by the sea with my parents, do I? That means the rest of the time I can be around town and stay with my aunt. Get it?'

Zammo shrugged. Jonah's schemes sounded brilliant. But they usually ended in trouble for someone else.

'Supposing the school journey's to some dead boring place?'

'It won't be. Trust me. This is the answer to our prayers.'

'Yours, you mean.'

'What's the difference, if you can't share with your friends.'

'Get stuffed.'

'Samuel Maguire.' Miss Mooney's voice sounded from the front.

Zammo realised the room had gone quiet around him.

16

'I'll see you at break time. Meanwhile kindly step up here and hand out these forms.'

In 4H Dan Hopwood was dealing with a barrage of questions. At last he called a halt.

'What I suggest is that anyone who is interested in the idea of a trip abroad, let me know at break time. We might as well find that out for a start.'

'I reckon it's a load of rubbish,' burst out Suzanne.

'You speak for yourself,' responded Claire. 'I happen to think it's about time the school organised something decent instead of wasting time checking up on what we're wearing.'

'All right for you. But how many people can afford that kind of money?'

'Come on Suzanne,' said Stew encouragingly. 'There are ways of raising it.'

'Oh, yes,' snapped Suzanne. 'I can stand outside the school gate with a tin cup, can't I?'

'You don't have to go,' said Duane.

'That's great,' stormed Suzanne.

'All right, all right,' commanded Hopwood. 'We can talk it over, quietly. There are more ways of solving the problem than you think. Now you lot have English first two periods, don't you?'

The class gathered its gear together and filed out. Dan Hopwood went his way, but the scene with Suzanne was still in his mind. Suzanne's world was a very unjust place. She reacted violently, but he had to sympathise.

At lunch time, when the form was back in the classroom, he went quietly over to her: 'About the possible trip, Suzanne. Seriously would you like to go?'

She glanced up, cheeks flaming.

'Seriously, this school can emigrate for all I care.'

She slammed down the lid of her desk and walked out leaving Mr Hopwood with his mouth open.

Chapter 5

At the end of school Jonah and Zammo lingered on the pavement.

'Hey, Zammo. What do you really think about going on the school journey?'

Zammo shrugged. 'I don't know. I mean it all depends where we're going, doesn't it?'

'Not much. I couldn't care less as long as I don't have to go with my Mum and Dad.'

'So, I get to go on holiday with the school just 'cause you don't want to go with your parents?'

'Don't be like that. Thing is, if I go with them, I'll be away for four weeks.'

Zammo nodded. 'S'right. I'll think about it. Anyway, I'll have to see what my Mum and Dad are doing.'

'Do you want to go with them?'

Zammo grinned. 'I doubt it. They might just want me on the school journey. But what about yours?'

Jonah made a face. 'That's my problem. They're stuck on family holidays. We ought to be together, they reckon.'

'Could be embarrassing when you get to fifty.'

'Hey.' Jonah jerked his head and moved away from the pavement edge to stand behind one of the school gate posts.

'What's that?' Zammo followed, squinting to his right. He saw someone pass by. It was Gripper Stebson. Zammo took cover. But Stebson showed no sign of having seen them. He stood for a second on the pavement then crossed the road towards the Arndale.

Jonah let his breath go. 'That was near.'

Zammo nodded. 'Funny thing is,' he said, 'the Animal's been leaving people alone this term. Do you think he's gone off human flesh?'

'Wish I knew. If I knew what he was planning, I'd keep clear.'

'Too right. You know, the worst thing about him is the way he comes up close behind you, quietly, so you can't get away. It makes your hair curl, thinking about it.'

'Yeah, and the worst time is lunch break.'

'Right on. He has more time for it. He can pick his victim and work on 'em.'

'D'you know, Jonah, what we ought to do is keep behind him. Watch him, see what he's doing.'

'Like follow my leader? Hey think about it. Everybody walking behind Gripper and him wondering where we've all gone.'

'Tell you what'd be really hairy.'

'What?'

'If he started a mob. He's always been a loner, except for that creep Denny Rees. If he started a gang, that could get nasty.'

'Think he's got the brains for that?'

'Oh, don't sell him short. He's cunning. He's got no feeling. That doesn't mean he's got no sense.'

'Anyway, I'm off home. Coming?'

'No, I've got to meet my Mum in the shopping centre. I'm getting new shoes.'

'Lucky boy. See you.'

'See you.'

When Jonah got home he was later than he thought. Dad was already there and tea on the table. Everybody seemed in a good mood. So he took the bull by the horns and broached the matter of the school journey.

'But, you're coming to the cottage with us,' said his mother. She sounded hurt.

'Where is this school trip?' demanded his father. Jonah didn't like the tone of his voice.

'I don't know. They haven't said, yet.'

'Well, how do you know you're going to like it better than where we're going?' asked his mother.

19

Jonah knew better than answer a question like that. He felt himself go slightly red and looked down at his plate. His Dad was annoyed. He could feel it in waves across the table.

'What you mean is you don't want to come with us, isn't it? Well, that's not on. The school trip can't be more than a fortnight. What'll you do for the rest of the time?'

'I'll stay with my Aunt Sandra,' said Jonah.

'You mean, hang around the streets with that Maguire lad, don't you?' His Dad's voice rose. 'I saw you messing about by the school gate when I was on my way home.'

Mrs Jones signalled to her husband but he had the bit between his teeth. 'I don't wonder your school report says you don't work hard enough. You spend too much time messing about with kids who have no ideas, kids who are going nowhere.'

Jonah raised his head.

'There's nothing wrong with Zammo.'

'Who?'

'He means Samuel,' said Mrs Jones soothingly. She sighed to herself. Nice family tea was turning into nice family row.

'Look, finish your tea, love. We'll talk about this another time.'

'As far as I'm concerned,' snapped Jonah's father, 'there's nothing more to discuss. He's coming with us.'

Chapter 6

In a side street near the shopping centre, Gripper Stebson gazed silently into the window of a small shop. The window was grubby, the items on display were grubby. But he found them fascinating.

One half of the display was taken up with illustrated books and magazines from the last war. Their lurid covers showed scenes of death and destruction. Iron-jawed soldiers, steel helmets aslant on their heads, plunged bayonets into the cringing bodies of their enemies. Blond giants, black leather caps on massive heads, pointed from the open turrets of tanks as they crushed their way over corpses and rubble.

On the other side of the window was the hardware, daggers in tooled scabbards, iron crosses with ribbons spilling from faded plush mountings, half-sheathed bayonets, model pistols, armbands with black swastika symbols. It was a jumble of stuff, the kind of thing that appealed to ancient creeps with more money than sense and younger ones with too much bone between the ears.

But Gripper did not belong to either group. He was looking for something. He had an idea. Zammo had read his thoughts. He was about to launch a company, a small band of like minds. He had already picked them. He hadn't told them yet. But he did not expect any refusals for his offer. He wouldn't take any either.

In the past year, Gripper had had one or two disagreeable experiences. He had run up against people, like Jenkins and Humphreys who were bigger than he was. It had been humiliating. It was not going to happen again. Now Jenkins and Co were no longer at Grange Hill. They were out in the world looking for jobs.

But there would be other Robin Hoods who could interfere with his trade and had the muscle to do so. Every time it happened, those smaller than Stebson seemed to get more impudent. He intended to alter that. That was why G. Stebson was going public.

Right now what he wanted was a means of identification.

Something to mark out the members of his outfit without attracting the attention of interfering members of staff. Hopwood, for example, was waiting for the chance to bounce him right out of Grange Hill. That would be very bad. It would take time to get the business going again in a new school. So he was planning ahead.

He had now found what he wanted. It lay in the window, a narrow red and white armband with a swastika badge inside a black circle. Stitched inside the sleeve of a bomber jacket, hidden from prying eyes, revealed at the twist of a cuff, it had all the ambitious thug needed. But they did not come cheap. He needed six of them. It would cost nearly twenty quid. But he wanted them in his hand first. The other club members could pay for them on issue, at a profit for G. Stebson. But that came later.

Deep in thought he almost bumped into a Grange Hill boy as he turned away from the window. He recognised him in a flash. It was Maguire, one of the few in the lower school who was not rigid with fear of Gripper. But Stebson controlled himself. Maguire was with his mother. And Mrs Maguire looked the kind of person who could see off a small regiment of Stebsons. He brushed past them.

Zammo stopped by the small shop window and looked in. His mother jerked his sleeve.

'Come on son, what do you want with that rubbish?'

'Nothing Mum,' answered Zammo, truthfully.

But what did Gripper want with it?

Chapter 7

One lunch time later that week, the School Journey Committee held its first meeting. Present were Baxter, Hopwood, Miss Lexington Miss Mooney, Sutcliffe and McGuffey. McGuffey had found himself, somewhat to his surprise, elected secretary.

As Baxter told him frankly: 'You are the youngest. The experience will do you good. On the other hand the willing chap always gets smiled on by the Governors when it comes to promotion. If all goes well, the troops will love you, too.'

'And, if all goes badly,' asked McGuffey.

'Then,' replied Baxter, cheerfully, 'it's the fault of the travel agent.'

'I saw this article,' remarked Miss Lexington, 'from a travel agent who said he was thinking of leaving the profession, because school journeys were wearing him down.'

'True,' added Hopwood, 'I believe some firms are asking schools to insure against claims for damage on school trips.'

'Oh, they'll be thinking of Eton and Harrow, not Grange Hill,' said Baxter. 'But if we are talking about horror stories, I could a few unfold: like double booking: you arrive with fifty tired and hungry kids and find a Mexican High School are sleeping in your beds. Or the coach you have hired breaks down fifty miles away from the hotel.'

'Or surcharges, there's another thing . . .'

'Oh, we all know about this . . . let's get on with it,' demanded Miss Mooney.

'There's only one real question,' answered Hopwood. 'That's where?'

'How about: how much?'

'I thought that was decided already. £150 ceiling.'

'Even that's too much for some.'

'Well, let's leave the impossible and work on the difficult one. Where?'

Hopwood dropped a pile of brochures on the floor.

'I've been looking through these. No, they're not for general reading. I'll tell you what the possibilities are. I've ruled out work holidays because they cut out the under 14's. Ski-ing's out because we're too late. Camping too because the last trip we had was a camp one.'

'You can say that again.'

'Thank you. Cruises cost too much. We haven't time to raise the money. So it looks like a big city stay . . .'

Baxter shuddered: 'Museums . . .'

Hopwood went on: 'River cruise, town to town coach tour, or stay in one small country spot and explore.'

'Which countries?'

'We've thirty to choose from, from what I can see.'

'Come on, Dan. There are really only half a dozen within easy reach.' Miss Lexington held up her hand: 'France, Germany, Spain, Belgium, Holland . . .'

'We can get five days in the Rhineland for £80.'

'Too short.'

'Budget air tour for £100 – no, that's March and April only.'

'Ten days in Switzerland for £130.'

'Let's have a look at that one. The coach tours have it over air for cheapness, but this one is ten days of which four or five are on the road in different hotels – only have the time on the spot.'

'I like that, keep 'em on the move. They don't get bored.'

'I don't, too tiring,' came several voices.

'Are you thinking of yourselves or the kids?' demanded Miss Mooney. There was a sudden silence.

'Come on, Terri,' said Graham Sutcliffe. 'It's our holiday as well.'

'Oh yes. And how do we justify the free places – unless we're working?'

'Children, children,' interrupted Baxter. 'Incidentally, what is the market in free places on these coach trips?'

'Oh, it varies from three per twenty pupils to one for every six. If we have fifty on this trip, no more, we would get seven free places.'

'We could do with eight adults, I reckon.'

'Well that we can cover by pooling.'

'So,' said Hopwood, 'what shall it be: coach or air, and where?'

'I favour air, a ten day trip gives us nearly nine days on the spot, cuts down the journey hassle,' said Baxter.

He looked round: 'That agreed?' He turned to McGuffey. 'We'll need some quotations quickly.'

'There is one possibility,' said Sutcliffe. 'We act as our own agents – make up our own package and get an operator to quote for that.'

'One thing at a time,' put in Hopwood as a look of panic spread over McGuffey's face.

Baxter nodded. 'One thing at a time it is. Let's meet again this time next week . . .'

'We must do something about finding one or two more adults, women in particular.'

There was a silence.

'We are all we have. It's a bad year for volunteers.'

'I think I may have the solution,' said Hopwood. 'Pamela Cartwright, doing a year at a play centre, before going to college. Very sports orientated, good with younger kids.'

'Won't she have a holiday lined up already, with a boy friend?'

'She could bring him along and split the free place.'

'Depends who it is.'

'Oh, it'll be someone reliable, knowing Pamela.'

Chapter 8

But not only the Holiday Think Tank was at work.

Next morning, as the Grange Hill pupils streamed into school, Mr Keating had to break up a large pushing, laughing mob around the main notice board. There in full view was a large poster with a tasteful potato cut border. In the middle in neat lettering was an announcement:

MCGUFFEY'S TOURS

Have a cheap holiday with Grange Hill. See the world.
Work your way.
One week with the guerillas in El Salvador.
Ten days picketing in Warsaw with Solidarity.
A riotous week in the streets of Brixton.
Contact your organiser.
It's a revolution in holiday thinking.

Mr Keating smartly removed the notice amid groans of disgust. He took it to the Head's office. Mrs McCluskey was not amused.

'Someone is trying to discredit the whole scheme.'

'Oh, I hope not,' he said smoothly. 'Rather a joke at Mr McGuffey's expense, I thought, and quite witty.'

'Witty, yes. Funny, no. It all points to the fact that we must hurry up and decide where the school journey is going.'

Mr Keating coughed: 'It might have been better to have decided that before the news got out.'

The Head glared: 'That is a mystery to me: how something discussed at a Governors' meeting can be known by every first year inside twenty-four hours.'

'Well you know, the only ones who know everything

about a school are the pupils. They are everywhere. We can't be.'

'Hm. Well we shall have to see if we can catch the phantom pamphleteer quickly. In the mean time, I shall see Mr McGuffey and see if we can speed up certain other matters.'

Chapter 9

Hopwood looked at the circle of faces around his desk.

'No, I'm sorry. I can't tell you where we shall be going. But it will cost around £150. We'll start a savings scheme. Meanwhile you could think of money-raising ideas yourself.'

'Like sponsorship, sir,' asked Pogo Patterson, quickly shifting the lump of chocolate across his mouth.

Hopwood grinned.

'You could give up Mars bars for a year. That should raise a bit.'

'That'd ruin the firm,' said Duane.

'Not a bad idea, though,' put in Claire. 'A sponsored slim.'

'Hey, that's it Pogo. Ten p for every pound you lose.'

'Yeah, if we all chipped in, maybe he'd disappear.'

Pogo glared at them. 'Who says I want to go abroad with you mob anyway?'

'Be like that.'

'I think this sponsoring business is stupid,' said Suzanne, 'going around with collecting sheets begging money.'

'Well, you don't have to raise money in the school, if it embarrasses you,' retorted Claire.

'Embarrasses me!' exploded Suzanne. 'The whole blo – ' she looked at Hopwood and put a hand to her mouth. 'This whole school journey lark is ridiculous, can't even make up their minds where we're going.'

'Mr McGuffey can,' said Duane. The circle started to laugh.

Hopwood frowned. 'Now if we're talking about stupidity, that bit of flyposting was stupid. Mr McGuffey and other people are doing their best to organise a holiday and someone seems to be trying to sabotage it.'

'I can't see anything wrong with that poster,' said

28

Suzanne, defiantly. Hopwood looked up from his desk and caught her eye.

Just as quickly Suzanne looked away again, then turned and marched back to her desk.

The group around Mr Hopwood broke up. He frowned to himself. Something was nagging at the back of his mind.

* * *

HEARD ON THE PHONE

'Hello Susi.'

'Hello Pam.'

'Have you made up your mind about summer holidays yet?'

'Not yet.'

'How'd you like to go back to Grange Hill?'

'Pull the other one. What are you raving about?'

'They are taking fifty kiddiwinkies abroad. There are two free places for young adults. It's YOP with a difference. That is where we come in.'

'How about Alan?'

'Bring him along. You can split your free place with him. So he gets a cheap holiday too.'

'What about you? Have you asked Mr Jenkins?'

'I have.'

'What did he say?'

'He laughed.'

'That makes the score one all, then.'

'It does. But I'll work on him. You work on Alan.'

'OK. What can I lose?'

Chapter 10

LEXINGTON TOURS

All girls' trip to volcanic regions of Iceland.
Special attention to hot geezers.

The crowd round the notice board split up as Baxter moved in and pulled the latest holiday 'announcement' down.

'Aw, sir, leave it up. That one was good,' said Annette.

'Nonsense child. Most unhealthy, reading things like this,' and Baxter marched away swiftly before the pupils could see the grin at the corner of his mouth. He wheeled into the staffroom and flung the poster on the table.

'Whoever is doing it, certainly has the touch,' he said.

Miss Lexington examined the paper.

'Whoever is doing it must be a sexist pig like yourself, Geoff.'

'Oh no,' Miss Mooney studied the notice. 'That's no man's work. The typing is impeccable. A credit to the Commerce Department.'

'Who's being sexist now?' demanded Sutcliffe from across the room. 'There's no guarantee a girl did that. It could be someone like Stebson trying to disrupt things generally.'

'Graham, you are not seriously suggesting anything as witty and well spelt as that could come from the Mr Hyde of 4H are you?'

Sutcliffe shrugged: 'Stebson has friends.'

'Friends?'

'We-ell. I have noticed that lately he has abandoned his lone wolf role and begun to assemble a gang.'

'Ah, that could be bad news. Must keep an eye on that. But

this leaflet shows a higher intelligence, if not more responsibility.'

'You're right, Geoff,' said Dan Hopwood, 'and I think I know who.'

'Aha.'

'Yes. No names, no pack drill.'

Someone else had the same idea.

At lunch break Hopwood was asked to see the Head. She came to the point straight away.

'I've been talking to the Head of Commerce. It does seem likely that Suzanne Ross has been producing these offensive posters.'

'How?'

'Bits and pieces of typing found by the desk she had been using.'

Hopwood was indignant.

'That sounds like snooping.'

The Head frowned.

'Nothing of the sort. It was – accidental. Now I think we must decide what to do about that young lady. After her behaviour last year, plus her absenteeism, she had come close to suspension. I think she has overstepped the mark.'

Hopwood shook his head.

'Suzanne has been something of a trial. But in this case she does have a point.'

'A point?' The Head's voice rose.

'I think it is a sort of protest about the school journey. She has been complaining about the cost. Her family cannot really afford it.'

'Lots of families cannot afford things. But I do not see how we can help in this case.'

'So you mean the less well-off are to be excluded?'

'You know I do not mean that, Mr Hopwood. If there were some way we could help discreetly.'

'Discreet help would send Suzanne up the wall. We have to find some way of helping that is fair all round. Some form of joint sponsorship.'

'Mr Hopwood. I do not see the whole school being

involved in a scheme to soothe the hurt feelings of one obstreperous young lady.'

She paused.

'Particularly at a time when the staff are apparently about to set arbitrary limits on what they will do and what they will not do for the school.'

'If you are referring to staff industrial action, then that is something I would prefer to discuss with you on another occasion – and perhaps more formally.' Mr Hopwood's voice was cool. The Head nodded.

'Quite so. But what about Suzanne?'

'Let me try dropping a hint to her. And at the same time I will try and work something out.'

'Very well. But I hope she will take the hint. Otherwise . . .' The Head left the sentence unfinished.

Chapter 11

McGuffey looked round helplessly at the other staff gathered in a corner of the staff room. The floor in front of him was strewn with brochures.

'It was here,' he said.

'What's that in your shirt pocket?' Miss Mooney extended a sympathetic finger.

'Can't be that. I put it with the other papers.' He turned red. 'Oh yes. Here we are.'

'At the moment it's coach or rail. Ten days with the kind of air package we can get for our size of group is nearer £200 than £150.'

'You've tried . . . ?'

'I've tried everywhere.' McGuffey was irritated and the question was never completed.

'Look, I'm beginning to get just the slightest bit bored with this exercise.'

'Come on now.'

'Come on nothing. One day we're in a union meeting saying we have got to lighten this workload somehow. Next day we have a jolly get together to see how much more we can do.'

'Well, I think . . .' began Miss Mooney. Then she stopped as Hopwood came into the room, face angry. 'What's wrong, Dan?'

'Ah, just the Boss having a go at me about the union.'

'Oh, that was a bit uncalled for.'

'Yes – right at the end of a discussion about something else.'

'She's smart, you know.'

'She may be. She is also very nervous. If there is a withdrawal of goodwill things could get heavy. She's spent two years letting it be known she runs a very tight ship.'

'Well, it's time the stokers spoke up.'

Dan Hopwood turned to the last speaker.

'All very well to talk, but I'm the one who carries the can, remember?'

Baxter interrupted hastily.

'We were discussing holidays you remember.'

'Yes we were, but the news is no better on that front.'

'Oh.'

McGuffey explained the position. Hopwood drew in a deep breath. 'Just what we needed!'

'Let us get a cup of tea and brood for a while.'

Five minutes later the group was still sitting in silence when Miss Lexington came smartly into the room followed by a young man slender in build, fairhaired and sunburnt.

'I hope you haven't taken any big decision about the school journey yet?'

She was greeted by groans and laughter.

'Only that it would be simpler to take them on a Magical Mystery Tour of the next Borough.'

'Oh, like that. No – I, or rather Rolf and I think we have the solution.'

Chapter 12

All turned and looked at the young man who began to go slightly pink. Miss Lexington intervened.

'You know Rolf is on a year's exchange. Well, we were chatting today about holidays in Italy, that's why I'm a bit late. Anyway, we had this tremendous idea.'

'What, a school journey to Italy?'

'No, Austria.'

'Ah, that figures.'

'Actually,' the young man put in, 'it is the Tyrol.'

'Aha, the mountains,' said Sutcliffe. 'Grange Hills are alive . . .'

'Graham, be serious a moment,' said Terri Mooney. She turned to Rolf. 'We are all getting a bit hysterical about this journey.'

'At home, we used to go for summer and winter holidays to this valley in the Unterberg . . .'

'Where's that?'

'Well, that's a general name for the lower part of the River Inn. It's a lovely valley called Ellertal. Quite isolated.' He took a quick look round. 'But not too isolated. We often stayed at a farm, the Schindlerhof, at the head of the valley. At one time Herr Schindler was renowned for training horses. Since he died Frau Schindler has closed the stables and turned the farm partly into a hostel for school students.'

Miss Lexington interrupted: 'The thing is she charges only student rates, full board, packed lunches. Her son, Friedl, is a fully trained guide. The whole family helps. It could be ideal.'

Baxter pursed his lips: 'How do we get in? Surely she will be booked up.'

'Ah, that's it,' Rolf grinned: 'On the other side of the

village road, is another establishment run by Frau Becker. They are – as you might say – rivals of a kind.

'This August, for some reason, the school who would normally stay with Frau Schindler, has transferred to Frau Becker.'

'Aha, something funny in the schnitzel?'

Rolf frowned. 'Frau Schindler is an excellent cook,' he said stiffly.

'So, if we stay at Schindlers, what do we give the troops?'

'Hiking, swimming, excursions, Salzburg, Innsbruck, the Mozart House.'

'Ah, museums. Say no more.'

'It sounds all right to me,' said Miss Lexington. 'Walk them up and down the hills, tire them out, have them in bed by ten o'clock worn out and things could not be better.'

'Right. What we need to do is work out how much the total package is with air fares.'

'We'll need to allow for booking coaches for excursions.'

'And, there's passports.'

'Some of the kids already have passports. Group passport will cover the rest.'

'Don't you need identity cards for Austria?'

'Boots, walking shoes, haversacks.'

Everyone turned to McGuffey.

'Made a note of all that?' asked Baxter cheerfully. But McGuffey was looking under the table.

'I've lost that bit of paper with the air fares,' he said plaintively.

Chapter 13

The morning crowd milled around the notice board.

'Austrian Alps – Ellertal – never heard of it.'

'Course you have. Tyrol. That's where they did *Sound of Music*.'

'Oh no, I'm not spending summer with a load of nuns.'

'I reckon it's a joke – like those others.'

'No, it's not. It says contact Mr McGuffey.'

'So?'

'Well, I can prove it's no joke.'

'How?'

'It says ten pound deposit.'

'Right – it does. And it says here – riding stables. I'm not sleeping on straw with a lot of horses for £150.'

'Who says the horses'd have you?'

'You know what we'll be doing. Marching up and down hills yodelling all day.'

'It says day trips to places.'

'Like what?'

'Well, there's salt mines.'

'We could leave a few behind there.'

'And Salzburg – the Mozart House.'

'Who's he?'

'You don't know Mozart – you ignorant pig? He beat Hurricane Higgins in the snooker finals.'

'He's a musician, brick-brain.'

'What group's he in then?'

'He's not in a group, he's dead.'

'Thrills. Now, if you'd said Dracula.'

As the group split up and Miss Mooney's form filed into their room, Fay said to Annette, 'You know, I think I'll go after all.'

Annette stared: 'You'll go. What's changed your tune?'

'Have you seen? Rolf Whatsits going to be there. He's running German conversation classes at lunch time.'

'Don't be stupid. We're going to Austria.'

'You are dim, you know. They speak German in Austria.'

'But you don't do German.'

'I know,' said Fay, brushing her nails gently on her lapels. 'But I could make an effort for Rolf. He's terrific.'

Annette looked at her sharply.

'You know, you're crazy about blokes, aren't you?'

'Who's talking? Who's always messing about with lads, throwing snowballs, stuffing paper clips down their necks?'

'That's different. That's fun. Girls are so wet at times.'

'That's what I mean. Boys are more interesting.'

'Yeah, but the way you moon around after them's a real drag.'

'And the way you play up to them's disgusting.'

Miss Mooney thumped on her table.

'Annette and Fay, will you keep your private fight for your spare time. Now those of you who are going on the trip, collect your forms. And there's a note for your parents. We shall invite them to a meeting to explain all about it.' She stopped in her handing out of the papers and said, 'Weren't you on the list, Jones?'

'Oh no, Miss. My parents want me to go with them.'

'Oh, that's a pity.'

'I'm not worried,' said Jonah.

As Miss Mooney went back to her desk, Zammo turned to Jonah and demanded: 'What do you mean? You're not worried. You were choked the other day.'

'That was the other day – not now. Catch me climbing up and down hills with a lot of geezers in leather shorts. My names not Julie Andrews.'

'Don't know. Could be interesting.'

'Interesting? You're off your rails.'

Zammo turned to Jonah.

'Well it could be a sight more interesting than messing about round home. Anyway, what difference does it make to you? You'll be away with your Mum and Dad.'

'Suppose they change their minds.'

'Look mate. I can't keep up with you.'

'Quiet at the back there,' came Miss Mooney's voice.

When Jonah reached home that evening, his mother greeted him with a smile. 'Your father and I have been talking it over. We think it would be a good idea for you to have a holiday on your own for once. You can go on the school journey.'

Jonah thought quickly. 'I don't want to go on the school journey. I've changed my mind.'

'Oh, you mean you want to come with us. That's nice.'

'We-ell, no Mum, I'd just as soon stay here. I mean stay with my Aunt. Er – can I use the phone?' He had to reach Zammo before he got himself fixed up to go on that flipping mountain lark. Suddenly life was very complicated.

No it wasn't.

From the kitchen came Dad's voice: 'Either you come with us or you go on the school journey. You are not messing round the streets with that Maguire lad.'

'But I think he's going on the school journey, Dad.'

'Well, it'll do you both a bit of good, then,' said Mr Jones, and got on with his tea.

'We'll get you a new pair of climbing boots,' said his mother.

* * *

HEARD ON THE PHONE

'That you Alan?'

'Yeah, Tucker.'

'Listen, I want a rucksack.'

'You can get treatment for that.'

'Have you got one?'

'I have.'

'Can I have it?'

'No, I'm using it.'

'What for?'

'I'm going hiking, aren't I?'

'You, where?'

'Up the yodel belt. Austrian Alps, mate.'

'I don't believe it.'

'You'd better.'

'Who with?'

'Well, Susi for starters, and – a small party.'

'You can get done for that, mate. Who?'

'Like Grange Hill.'

'Hello Tucker . . . you still there?'

'Yeah.'

'You're coming as well, aren't you, with Cartwright.'

'Yeah, what's so funny?'

'I thought Cartwright was riding pillion into the Great Beyond on a Bonny borrowed from somebody's cousin.'

'Oh no, that's all wrong.'

'How?'

'Well my cousin only wrote off his Bonny, didn't he?'

'Get off, where? On the M1?'

'No, he went into that bike shop up the High Road.'

'Well, what was wrong with that?'

'He was on his iron, wasn't he?'

'Hey, Tucker, let me guess. Was he insured?'

'No comment.'

'Tucker. Someone I know has had a lucky escape.'

'You could be right. Listen, Alan.'

'I'm listening.'

'When we get there, we share a room, right?'

'Yeah?'

'OK, make sure ours is next to theirs.'

'Oh mate, you don't know Susi MacMahon.'

'Yeah, but I know Cartwright.'

'Famous last words. Tell you what, Tucker. I know a bloke who's got a spare rucksack.'

'Is he insured?'

Chapter 14

Gripper Stebson stood by the shop window in the dusk. Spring was near but it was still cold. He dug his hands deeper into his bomber jacket and blew through his teeth. He was on the point of going in to buy his armbands. He'd picked his six men. But one thing made him pause. Armbands were all right for them. Those who were taking the orders. But he needed something different for himself, since he'd be giving them. He needed something with a touch of class, something with a meaning he'd have to explain to them. Something they couldn't get even if they tried. Something they couldn't buy. A one off. And that he couldn't find.

But he didn't want to start asking in the shop. Asking meant telling and he wasn't telling. He had to spot what he wanted. When he did he would know.

'Lot of rubbish.'

Gripper turned. The voice was at his elbow. It was a little bloke, old. He just came up to Gripper's shoulder, but that was enough. His breath stank. He spoke again. A line of white foam appeared on his lips.

'Load of rubbish. Made in bloody Birmingham, those pistols. And those SS armbands, made in Hong Kong.'

He grabbed Gripper's arm. Gripper moved away, but the hold was too strong.

'Not authentic. If every bit of ex-Nazi gear in these shops was real, there would have been about two hundred million Nazis, wouldn't there? I wouldn't give ten bob for that lot.'

'So?' Gripper was uneasy, but fascinated. The little man came closer. Cropped white hair showed under his greasy cloth cap.

'The real stuff you can only get on-the-spot.'

'Where?' Gripper spoke in spite of himself.

'In the war, son, in the war. Taken off Jerries who've been killed. Lots of stuff brought back you know, machine pistols, Lugers. Secret stuff.'

'Listen, my place is just round the corner. I'll show you some real gear.'

Gripper's lip curled. What an old scumbag. Then he shrugged. Why not? He could look after himself.

'OK.'

The old man lived in a flat at the top of a battered tower block beyond the shopping centre. There was no lift working. They climbed five flights of stairs, but the old man talked all the way, breathlessly spraying Gripper's face as he spoke. They passed through a dark, dankly smelling kitchen and the old man fumbled with some keys.

'Can't trust 'em round here.'

The inner door was flung open. A light switch clicked. The room was filled with fluorescent lighting and Gripper stared in amazement. It was packed from floor to ceiling with gear. Not in a jumble, but laid out like a museum, crossed bayonets, pistols, hand grenades, small banners with tasselled cords, medals and badges set on baize panels, iron crosses, swastika emblems. In a corner a huge poster showed a young giant in grey uniform holding a banner.

Der sieg wird unsere sein.

'What's that?'

'Victory will be ours,' gabbled the old man. 'But it wasn't was it? The Russkis screwed them didn't they. They had to be tough to screw that lot, the Waffen SS.'

His eyes gleamed.

'The Waffen SS, they were real – bastards.'

He took hold of Gripper's jacket.

'But they weren't the worst. The toughest of the lot were the ones who were the Condor Legion.'

The old bloke's eyes seemed to cross. His voice sounded far away.

'That's one I haven't got. A Condor Legion badge. No one's got one of them.'

Gripper jerked away and turned to another wall, half covered with an enormous map. The old man stumbled after him, and pressed a switch. The map lit up. 'That's Munich. Where Hitler started it all. There's lots of 'em there still. I was over there for one of those Beer Festivals. I met some of the old uns. But I never found anybody from the Condor Legion.'

He pointed. 'Look, that's Berchtesgaden. That's where Hitler had his hideout and his treasure. Up in the mountains. And that's the Tyrol, all the way down to Italy. That's the Brenner Pass. That's where Hitler met Mussolini.'

'Tyrol?' asked Gripper.

The old man didn't hear him. He was still gabbling on when Gripper felt his way through the dark kitchen and out into the street.

Chapter 15

'How are we doing so far?' asked Baxter as he sat, tea mug in hand, in the staffroom. He looked out of the window. 'The birds are nesting. Buds are forming. Time's getting on.'

'Well,' said Hopwood, 'the list is closed. Fifty-two signed on. Deposits paid. Savings schemes started. And some ingenious money raising schemes on the go.'

'Like?'

'Douglas Patterson asks us to sponsor him ten p for every pound in weight he loses between now and when we set sail. He's lost a lot of weight already, but there's still some way to go.'

'Yes,' added Terri Mooney, 'and Samuel Maguire aims to break the world record for keeping a ball in the air without a bounce – 20p a hundred bounces or kicks or something.'

'Stewart has some scheme lined up with the computer, guessing multiples to within a hundred.'

'Very ingenious, as you say,' murmured Baxter, 'but so far, they seem to be collecting largely from each other, like taking in each other's washing.'

'Yes, and they're all collecting from us,' muttered Sutcliffe.

'What does it matter, as long as they are organising something.'

'Well, I think we should think of some way of co-ordinating the effort,' said Hopwood. 'Some people are still being left out.'

'Oh, Suzanne making trouble still?'

'Well, yes and no. She doesn't say much.'

'Those comic posters have stopped appearing, haven't they?'

'Oh yes. I had a quiet word with Suzanne. Dropped a broad hint. I also persuaded her to come on the holiday, if we could find some way of helping. Just how one can do that without singling people out, I cannot say. The Head's dead against using the School Fund.'

'No council grants going?'

'No indeed. They won't even pay our wages next year.'

'Don't start that again, please Dan.'

'OK. The best thing going though is Rolf's German language club. Thirty people every Wednesday lunch time, roars of laughter as I came past the room, plays on words like noodle and yodel, kissen and kussen, wirgl and worzel. Sounded like dirty Alpine jokes to me.'

'Yes and guess who's joined the club?'

'Who?'

'One Gripper Stebson.'

'Mugging up on his German, no doubt.'

'Ho ho. No, apparently asking intriguing questions about geography and history.'

'I smell a rat.'

'Anyway, he's signed up, paid his deposit.'

'If he starts a sponsor sheet, then we can start worrying.'

'Since you mention it,' said Terri Mooney, 'I do worry. I'm not sure he should have been allowed on the trip. Some of the First Years are terrified of him.'

'I think we have the antidote, Terri.'

'Oh?'

'Yes. I told you Pamela Cartwright is coming with us. Well Peter Jenkins is riding shotgun. He will keep Stebson in order.'

'Won't he create some disorder himself?'

'Come on, Geoff. Peter is the soul of discretion these days. A mature personality.'

'Yes, that's what worries me. The mature bit.'

'That is Ms Cartwright's problem. Now we are all set now, with all problems solved.'

'Well, since you ask, they aren't.' All stared at the anger in McGuffey's voice.

'Yes, as it happens. We still have a transport problem.'

'How do you mean? We can't get air passage?'

'What have you been playing at, man?'

McGuffey threw down his papers.

'What I mean is that the cost still puts us £15 to £20 outside our target figure. And that would rule out a number of people, not just Suzanne.'

'Any ideas on what to do?'

'Since you ask, I have. If all the free tickets were pooled we could cut the cost by sixteen per cent.'

'Gently, Bentley,' said Baxter. 'You want people to work and pay for their holiday as well? What was that we heard from you the other night about too many demands being made on teachers?'

Hopwood intervened hastily. 'Geoff, let's leave it. We'll all have to get stuck in and find a solution to this problem. I'm sure there's a way.'

Chapter 16

Not only had G. Stebson signed up for the school journey.
Not only was he studying German in Rolf's language club.
He had also embarked on a money raising scheme. He had a
sponsor sheet. It was a very successful sponsor sheet. It had
names on it with sums they had agreed to pay. What it did
not say was what feat Gripper would perform in return for
his sponsor money. But since each sponsor knew what feats
he could perform if need be, no questions were asked. He
went about his work quietly and with the minimum of fuss.

He had signed up Douglas Patterson for ten per cent of
what he raised on his slimming campaign. This was bad
enough, but the news was indeed worse. Douglas had not
told Gripper that in fact he was not slimming but putting on
weight. By the holiday he reckoned he would be ten pounds
heavier, not lighter. Some people lose weight when they
worry. Pogo was one of those who worry and eat more to get
over it. He got fatter and more anxious as term went on.

Another candidate for Gripper's list was Zammo, for a
share of his fantastic football bouncing effort. Gripper still
had to catch up with Maguire and Jones though and he had
not worked out how, yet.

The fact of the matter was, they were keeping behind him,
not only in the short break, but during the long lunch hour. It
took planning, foresight, ingenuity, agility and luck. But
between them Jonah and Zammo had the first four qualities
and everyone is entitled to luck.

The problem with luck is that every now and then it runs
out. Zammo had a funny feeling, between his shoulder
blades at three in the morning sometime, that luck might run
out before long.

But as it happened, help was coming, from a strange
quarter.

Chapter 17

Though they did not know it, the teachers were taking a hand in the guerilla war between Stebson and his victims. At the close of school, that day, Grange Hill staff had a very important and very heated meeting. It had to do with salaries, with the insulting offer they had just received from their employers of three per cent or three pence in the pound for those not mathematically minded.

All were agreed it was insulting. All were agreed that the only polite answer was two stiff fingers. But what to do about it? There agreement broke down.

McGuffey was first on his feet as soon as Dan Hopwood declared the meeting open.

'We have got to make an impression. When we say withdraw goodwill we should mean it, sports events, meetings with parents, School fairs, dinner duties, everything we do and don't get paid for should be out.'

Miss Mooney was on her feet almost as soon as McGuffey was off his.

'The only people we shall be hurting that way are children and parents. I say we should not do anything to antagonise them. We should send another strong letter to the Education Committee. We have to think of the children.'

'All right, Florence Nightingale,' muttered McGuffey.

'Order, order,' said Dan Hopwood.

'Terri,' Miss Lexington spoke up. 'We do think of the kids. We think and talk about nothing else. Husbands, wives, friends, they are all sick of us rabbiting on about the school, the children. But more damage has been done to the kids by spending cuts than anything we will do. I think we should stop dinner duties just to let the powers that be see what the real situation is.'

'Pull out all stops, it's the only way,' came a voice from the back.

Baxter heaved himself out of his chair: 'How about stopping dinner duties *and* a letter to the Governors.'

He looked round: 'I am not making a cock up of our entry to the District Cup by pulling the plug out on sports events at this stage.'

'Why not?'

'Because I've committed myself. I never committed myself to be a baby minder when other people, including their parents, can eat their lunches in peace.'

'But teaching's different,' called Miss Mooney.

'And so's nursing Terri, and what do the nurses get – warm smiles and no cash.'

Dan Hopwood rose to his feet: 'We don't want a free for all.' He looked at McGuffey: 'Will you put a proposition?'

McGuffey nodded: 'I move that all unpaid, voluntary extra activities, everything dependent on goodwill, is barred.'

'Including the school journey?'

McGuffey flushed, swallowed, then said: 'If need be, yes.'

Hopwood turned to Miss Mooney and Baxter. 'Do you want to put your proposals to the vote?' They nodded.

'Any final points?'

'No, get on with it Dan, this meeting's unpaid overtime, you know.'

Hopwood raised his hand. 'Very well then, let's have it. First, the all-out proposition.'

The vote was soon over. McGuffey's proposal received ten votes, Miss Mooney's fifteen. Baxter's forty five.

'Very well, then,' said Hopwood. 'Dinner duties it is then, starting from Monday.'

'And what about the children?' asked Miss Mooney.

'They'll have to be locked out, poor things,' answered Baxter.

Chapter 18

'Lock them out?' Mrs McCluskey stared at Mr Keating. 'A thousand pupils at large around the neighbourhood, all lunch hour?'

'That is what it amounts to,' answered the Deputy Head. 'We are indeed under no obligation to take care of them during the lunch hour, you remember. It is a matter of public goodwill.'

He looked out of the Head's office window on to the school yard where Hopwood and Miss Lexington were on reception duty at the gate as the hordes streamed in for the start of the day.

'The staff feel they have to make their views known in no uncertain manner.'

'But it'll antagonise the public, the local shopkeepers.'

Keating cleared his throat. 'The shopkeepers do very well from our students' custom. I have a feeling they will do even better.'

'There are two weeks left before the holidays, almost anything could happen in ten working days.'

'I rather think the staff hope the powers that be will get the message before then.'

'And the governors. I have a meeting with them, next week. This is sure to be raised.'

'I think the staff will be raising it with the governors themselves. They really are very put out, Mrs McCluskey.'

The Head got up from her desk and paced to the window.

'They are not the only ones, Mr Keating.'

She paused next to him.

'Is there nothing we can do, short of this – lock out? Is it not possible to confine the children to one part of the school while senior staff supervise them?'

Mr Keating raised his hands.

'Oh goodness me no. I personally could not possibly do that.'

'But surely, you don't agree with these tactics?'

Mr Keating looked embarrassed. Then he faced the head, and spoke a little pompously.

'My personal point of view is not really relevant. I do not feel I should act in any way against my colleagues.'

'Well that's clear enough. Thank you very much, Mr Keating.'

Mr Keating took the last words to mean something like 'on your bike' and quietly left the room.

The Head stood for a moment in silence. Then she tapped the desk, took a deep breath. She made to sit down and begin her day's work, then stopped again. She paced up and down a couple of times.

The phone suddenly rang next door. She ignored it. It went on ringing. With an expression of annoyance, she suddenly remembered that her secretary was ill. The school bursar was not in today. The last economy cuts had put her on half time. The Head realised that she was running the ship on her own. She marched into the secretary's office and picked up the phone.

At first she could hear nothing. The window over the school yard was wide open, the noise from gathering clans was deafening. Putting the phone down she stepped to the window to close it then stopped, listening. Below her window two teachers were talking, she could not see who. Leaving the window open she returned to the desk, muttered, 'I'll call you back,' into the phone and came back to the listening post. The background noise was quieter now and the voices came more clearly.

'So old Keating wouldn't play ball?'

'Not he. He's an old prune sometimes but he knows the rule. Bridget's on her own now. No go-between any more.'

'Hm. Do her good. She ought to get out of that bunker of hers and find out what's going on in this school.'

Chapter 19

Mrs McCluskey worked at her desk for half an hour before the tension became too great. In that half hour she had been up and down like a yo-yo answering phones, dealing with queries, while trying to attend to her routine affairs and decide what to do about the withdrawal of goodwill. But the conversation she had overheard buzzed around her head like an angry fly. She knew it was fatal to think about people talking behind your back. But once you have heard them, you had to do something about it. Not that she would want to confront the two teachers, even if she were sure who had been talking. No, she was too old a war horse for that.

But that half-heard conversation, her small set-to with Keating, the annoying phone calls all combined to make her too restless to stay in her office. At last she got to her feet and went out into the passage. It was 9.30. There had been no assembly that morning and the customers were all at their lessons. Well, most of them. And likewise the teachers were all at their posts, or most of them.

Deep in thought Mrs McCluskey paced the school corridors. When one is deep in thought, one walks slowly, one walks quietly. And people do not hear one coming. So several people were taken by surprise.

Annette Firman, who had sneaked in late and was going by secret by-ways to her class making up her excuses as she went, was caught red handed and sent on her way with a flea in her ear and her name mentally noted by the Head. As she saw off Annette, the Head suddenly had a thought. She returned to her office and came out again with a small notebook and pencil. Back on her rounds she went, discreetly pacing the school's corridors and halls, exploring its many nooks and crannies.

There were many of them, she discovered, more of them than she was aware of.

The school was like a rabbit warren. And if she did not know all the little holes and corners, other people did. As she rounded the bend into one particular little inlet near the toilets she became aware of two people talking in whispers. At least one of them was talking in a whisper, while the other seemed to be too upset to do any talking at all, except a timid 'ye-es' now and then.

Behind the screen of the wall she saw the back of a close cropped bullet head and a pair of broad shoulders bursting out of their school uniform jacket. Beyond she could see the pale face and frightened eyes of a first year. Anyone in the know would have recognised the sight. It was Mr Stebson making someone an offer they could not refuse.

'Shouldn't you two be at your lessons?'

The little first year jumped like a shot rabbit and changed colour from white to pink. Gripper Stebson was more battle hardened. He turned, at first insolently, then more cautiously as he recognised the unfamiliar voice. Mrs McCluskey noticed money in the first year's hand. She frowned.

'What are you doing?'

Stebson thought quickly.

'I'm just collecting on my sponsor sheet, for the school journey,' he answered smoothly.

'Indeed, and where is the sheet?'

'It's with my gear in Mr Hopwood's room,' he said, remembering to add, 'Ma'am.'

'Ah, well perhaps your sponsor had better put his money away until you have it with you. Must do things correctly, mustn't we?'

She turned to the first year. 'Now off to where you should be, at the double.' The first year fled. Stebson was about to follow.

'Ah, you may wait a little bit. We don't want you falling over each other, do we?'

Twenty minutes later, Mrs McCluskey, feeling more at

53

ease with herself and the world, was back in her office, transferring several notes from her little book to her desk pad. She must remind Mr Thompson the caretaker about the window in the science block, still not repaired after four weeks. She must have a word with Mrs Taylor about leaving 3N unattended for ten minutes for no apparent reason. And she must get on to the county to have the floor in Mr Sutcliffe's room re-surfaced. The squealing and scraping of chairs on that threadbare surface was enough to drive anyone mad. It was amazing he put up with it.

When lunch time came, Mrs McCluskey, smiling like the Prime Minister on the Jimmy Young show, was at the school gate where the staff were seeing the troops on their way into the Great Outside. Mr Hopwood was busy with the padlock when she came up.

'If you wouldn't mind, Mr Hopwood, I'd like a brief word with you about one or two matters when school is over.'

He eyed her carefully, then said:

'Of course, Mrs McCluskey.'

Chapter 20

So the Great Lock Out began. And for a lot of people it soon became the Great Choke.

All kinds of persons who once were highly annoyed when they were not allowed out of school to go to the chippy and other important places, were suddenly choked to discover that they were being told to leave school.

Fay Lucas was choked because that meant she was missing German Club with Rolf who she had decided, much to Annette's disgust, was at least three notches more terrific than Mr Sutcliffe. Sooty was after all getting on a bit now and was practically married to Mooney.

Annette, of course, was delighted with the Great Lockout because all of a sudden there were a large number of entertaining annoyances to try out on a large number of people, and a large space to try them out in.

Stew was choked because he counted on lunch breaks to get on with the computer project he had taken on with Matthew Cartwright. Duane was choked because he felt the staff were pushing people around to suit themselves. Claire, though, was pleased because for once she felt free to spend her lunch hour as it suited her.

But of all the choked, the most choked, it had to be said was Gripper Stebson. Lunch hour was his tour of inspection time, the time when he did his minding and collecting. And suddenly the clientele was scattered to the four winds, around the parks, the shopping centre, the tower blocks, anywhere within a mile of the school, instead of being nicely boxed up for him to put the arm on.

This was noticed and very much appreciated by Zammo Maguire, who you'll remember, was in the middle of his GBS campaign. GBS, not for George Bernard Shaw, but for Get Behind Stebson, or rather keep behind Stebson. Zammo, somewhat to the narking of Jonah who preferred to sit on the wall in the sun with his take-away, was enjoying himself lurking around behind Gripper and keeping him under observation. He came back after lunch full of excitement. Gripper, it seemed, was assembling a task force in an old shed on a demolition site in the clearance area behind the shopping centre.

'Stebson's up to something,' he told Jonah. 'I'm going to suss out what it is.'

'You want your head attending to,' said his mate. 'Provided it stays on your shoulders.'

Other people were choked too. Park-keepers who suddenly had eight hundred more customers than they were used to; public lavatory attendants who did not find the additions to the graffiti on their walls the least bit amusing; flat dwellers who discovered the toy swings and roundabouts in the recreation area were being used by 12-stone fourth years; shop-keepers eager for custom but not eager to employ extra staff at lunch-times found themselves coping with fantastic queues.

Quite a few of this number looked up Grange Hill in the telephone directory. And guess who had to answer every phone call that came into the school that day?

Half way through the afternoon, Mrs McCluskey suddenly had the wicked impulse to refer all callers to Councillor Doyle on the Education Committee. But she restrained herself and soldiered on.

When she met Dan Hopwood at the close of play, she was so tense for a moment she forgot why she had arranged to meet him.

'Dan,' she said. Hopwood's eyebrows rose. The Head did not go much for Christian names. 'How long can this goodwill business last? It's creating havoc.'

He looked at her seriously: 'It is not our wish to start all this. If the Education Committee would give us some support, we would stop the action.' He paused: 'But that wasn't why you wanted to see me.'

'No. It's Stebson. I think I have seen his little extortion racket in action. He's using the school journey as a cover – and,' she suddenly grinned, 'I think I can see a way to stop it.'

Chapter 21

The end of term came nearer. The sun shone and every day the staff, at lunch time, turned out the customers to grass. By and by everyone settled down to a routine. The chippy man counted his cash and his blessings and ceased to ring up Mrs McCluskey. The people in the flats got the message (from someone) and began to ring up Councillor Doyle and annoy him. The council sent someone round to whitewash the walls of the public toilets, which is what the attendant had been trying to persuade them to do for years.

Gripper Stebson stopped trying to chase round the prairie trying to corral reluctant clients. Indeed, the word had got round the first years that Ma McCluskey had her beady eye on Gripper. Instead he gathered together with five or six chosen followers and plotted in dark corners, unaware that Zammo (disguised as Clark Kent) was keeping a close eye on him.

But there was more to come. One day, after school, Dan Hopwood assembled all the School Journey people and put a proposition to them.

'Money raising for an effort like this can be a problem for all of us, for some more than others.'

Out of the corner of his eye, he saw Suzanne's lip curl. But she kept silent and Hopwood went on.

'The Head and I, together with the other teachers involved in the journey, think it would be better if we all worked together. So she is prepared to lay on a special Saturday event at which everybody involved in the journey can perform, and raise money. Mr Baxter has suggested that he'll form a football team to play all comers – old boys' teams, parents' teams. We could have a talent competition and all the various sponsored activities can take place at once, in front of spectators.'

'Sir,' asked Claire, 'does that mean Patterson's going to be weighed in the nuddie to see if he's slimmed down?'

Hopwood grinned, then raised his hand to still the noise.

'It means everyone will put their talents on display.' He stopped a second and looked straight at Stebson, who looked him straight back in the eye.

'It means also that every sponsor sheet will have to be handed in, the amounts checked and registered. If we are going to go public on this one, it has to be fair and above board. Now I know what most of you with sponsor sheets have been planning but there are one or two of you who haven't let me know. How about Mr Stebson?'

Their eyes crossed again. Hopwood read Gripper's thoughts and was glad he was not superstitious.

'Yeah,' said Suzanne suddenly, 'I'd like to know what he's up to. I haven't even seen a list yet.'

'Yeah,' came a ragged chorus from all sides of the common room.

'I know you've started collecting, but we can soon regulate that. What activity will you lay on for us on the Day?'

For a second Gripper was at a loss, then Pogo spoke up, impulsively. 'He could run a circuit of the soccer pitch.'

'What?' demanded Claire, 'only one? Suppose he gets a quid a time? That's dead easy.'

Gripper turned as if he were about to dismantle Pogo and trade in the parts. Hopwood intervened.

'Let's say 25p a circuit.'

Gripper was silent. Then: 'I haven't got my list with me.'

'That's all right. We can make one out for you now. If you've forgotten how much people have contributed, they can let me know, can't they?' said Hopwood.

He opened his folder and watched by the other holiday makers, Gripper silently went to the front and was registered. It seemed he was in for a long run.

Chapter 22

As the school journey meeting was breaking up, Annette put up her hand.

'Sir,' she shouted, 'can you please ask the girls to hang on a minute, I've had a terrific idea.'

Hopwood grinned: 'We can ask. OK, folks, that's all. Will the ladies stay behind?'

'That's sex discrimination,' said Pogo.

'Huh,' retorted Claire. 'The day you stop being a sexist pig you can talk about sex discrimination.'

Pogo suddenly remembered that he had planned to slip away before Stebson called him in for service. He left the hall rapidly, as did most of the younger lads. Duane turned to Claire.

'You're not staying are you?' he demanded.

Claire hesitated. On the one hand it didn't suit her to take instructions from any second year like Annette. On the other hand she wasn't going to have Duane tell her whether she could stay or go. She struggled with herself for a moment, then said:

'Yeah, I'll stay. Hang about will you? I won't be long.'

While the girls gathered round Hopwood's table, the lads filtered out of the room, down the corridors and towards the school gate. Stebson, feeling thoroughly put out, went off on his own, Zammo and Jonah following him at a discreet distance.

Stew and Duane hung about by the school gate.

'They're having quite a meeting, aren't they? Wonder what they're planning.'

'Who cares?'

Stew stared at his mate: 'Hey what's got up your nose? There's no harm in it is there?'

'Ah,' Duane kicked a stone against the wall. 'She's always

60

messing me about. Hang about, she says. Who does she think she is?'

'Oh, like that?' said Stew. 'I'll change the subject.'

There was silence for a moment, then the sound of footsteps as a bunch of second years walked quickly out of the gate. Annette and Fay seemed to be having a row. They walked past the lads without even seeing them, talking at the tops of their voices.

'Well I think it was a stupid idea.'

'Please yourself, Fay, but at least keep it to yourself. If you let anybody know it'll spoil it.'

'Oh, I won't spoil it. You can't spoil anything that's rotten anyway.' She snorted with forced laughter.

'It might have been your idea to start with, but Claire's taken it over. You might have known they'd never agree to something thought up by lower school people.'

'Well, they did agree to it. They thought it was a good idea.'

'Yeah, if they were running it. And flipping Precious Matthews has to row in as well. She knows somebody that can fix it all up.'

'Well, so what, if she can, that's good isn't it.'

'Well I think it's crazy.'

Fay marched off across the road, Annette following her more slowly. Stewart looked at Duane.

'Claire's been narking everybody tonight, hasn't she?' He jerked his head. 'Here she comes now.'

Claire, with Suzanne and Precious, all talking excitedly, rushed past the two lads. Duane's mouth fell open. Claire stopped in her tracks and half turned.

'Sorry, got to see someone, urgently. Can't tell you what. It's confidential. See you tomorrow. Bye.'

Next moment they were gone, across the main road. Stew grinned.

'Come on, Duane, mate. Leave it. You can do the same to her some time.'

But Duane, face grim, muttered. 'She's not going to mess

me about like that. I'm going to find out what she's up to. She's going to be sorry.'

Duane walked off leaving Stew staring and raced across the road. The girls, yakking away, were now about twenty yards in front of him, too busy with their own affairs to notice the private eye behind them.

At the Arndale, they stopped abruptly and swung arm in arm to look in a boutique. Duane, taken by surprise, jerked to a stop. Someone coming up behind ran into him. Duane, now in a really nasty mood, turned to speak his mind, but stopped when he saw the bloke who'd ran into him was twice his size.

'Sorry,' he murmured, then he dodged into a shop entrance as the girls turned away from the window.

Next moment they were away again, so quickly he almost lost them, just catching sight of them through the glass of the shop where he was lurking. He kept them just in sight as they wound their way, joking and shrieking – they *were* having a jolly time – through the arcade. Then the noise stopped again. They had vanished.

Where had they gone? He hurried forward to reach the next corner. Then from the side of his eye he spotted something. He had come up to the curtained window of a small cafe. Over the curtain top he could see the three of them. Quickly he sheered away from the window and moved across the arcade. He could see them through the glass door of the cafe. One of them was on the phone now while the other two were drinking coffee. What were they up to? He felt stupid, hanging about here. But he wasn't going now till he found out something.

Ten minutes passed, then twenty. But Duane stuck to his post. Inside he could see the girls drinking coffee and giggling. Flaming women. All the – – . He heard footsteps in the arcade. Someone went past his watching post, then stopped, crossed the way and entered the cafe.

He stared. He knew that bloke. It was Benny Green, Jenkins' and Humphreys' mate. He'd left school last term.

What was he up to? Duane stared. Green was sitting down with the girls. Claire was getting him coffee. She put it on the table and tapped Green in a familiar sort of way on the shoulder before she sat down again. Duane suddenly felt a twinge in his stomach, something like sickness. It wasn't funny. He felt even more stupid. He knew he ought to pack it in and go home. It was all just some daft scheme they were working out. It had nothing to do with him. But why shouldn't she tell *him*? They were supposed to be – together. The way she'd just walked off, dismissed him, see you tomorrow (if I feel like it?).

In spite of himself, he stayed. The clock over the cafe curtains showed half past five already. He ought to go. But he hung on. Then the cafe door opened. He shrank back into his hiding place as Precious and Suzanne, calling out, 'See you', came out. Nobody followed them though. Inside Claire and Benny Green stayed at the table. They seemed to be bending over a piece of paper, a list of something.

It was getting on for six when they came out at last. The cafe was closing anyway. At the door Benny turned, put his hand on Claire's shoulder for a second (too long, thought Duane) and then moved off down the arcade. Claire, beaming all over her face, walked off in the opposite direction, Duane following miserably behind at twenty paces distance.

The other two sleuths lost their man, Gripper, at the foot of a tower block some half a mile away.

'Come on Zammo. No point waiting here. He could be all evening. You're wasting your time,' said Jonah.

Zammo shook his head.

'Don't you believe it. We've got to keep behind him – and one jump ahead,' he added as an afterthought.

Jonah stared, then slowly raised his right finger pointed it to his temple and revolved it.

'You know what's wrong with you?'

Chapter 23

Zammo was right, though. Gripper Stebson was up to something. He had assembled his recruits, six of them. But, though they did not know it, they were on probation. He wanted to see what they were made of before enrolling them in his company, armbands and all. And before going seriously into business he wanted to have his own badge of office to make clear to all concerned who was Number One. Ever since he'd met the old creep with his flat front room full of ex-Nazi loot, Gripper had thought more and more of the prospect of owning a Condor Legion badge, something nobody, but nobody else had.

And he had hopes that somehow, somewhere, on the school journey up in the Tyrol, he might find what he was looking for. The old man had assured him that during the summer, the Austrian Alps swarmed with tourists from Munich, and among them were not a few 'boys of the old brigade'. Gripper was sure that with a sharp eye and even sharper wits he might make the kind of contact which would mark him out.

Hence his keenness to join in Rolf's German Club. Not that Gripper had let out to anyone the reason for his linguistic ambitions. He did not even tell his newly assembled sonder-gruppe what he was after. Right now he was keen to see how they would perform.

The great Lock Out had put a stop to the German classes for a while. Which was another notch in Gripper's club as far as the Grange Hill staff were concerned. He was about to put a stick of dynamite under them, starting with little-friend-of-little-people D. Hopwood. So, in their shed bunker on the demolition site, they made their plans.

It was there that Zammo had spotted them and after a good deal of very risky snooping around, he worked out what they were up to. One lunch time he got close enough to see them up to it. Too close in face, for one of them spotted him and he had to run for his life. He set a new record for the one hundred metres. He moved so fast in fact that they didn't see who he was, though they knew he was a Grange Hill-ite.

Laughing, choking, breathless with running and excitement he burst into the chippy queue where Jonah and the others were patiently waiting their turn at the trough.

'Posters, mate, flipping posters.'

'And posters to you, too, Zammo,' murmured his friend.

'No, listen. They're going to march on the school. They've got placards with things like BAN RED TEACHERS, OPEN UP OUR SCHOOL.'

'Red teachers. What are they raving about? And what do they want the school opened up for? They don't want to work in their lunch hour, do they?'

'Who, like Stebson? Of course he wants to work in his lunch hour. And you know what he wants to work at.'

'Who he wants to work on, you mean.'

'I bet they'll try and bust the gate in.'

'Get off.'

'Hey,' Zammo punched his mate. 'I know what. Let's do a counter-demo.'

'What? Stebson'll total you.'

'No he won't. He won't be able to if he's running his own demo, will he? And not if the local paper's there, cameras and all, eh?'

'So what placards do we have: *I love teacher*? *I'm a good boy*? *Stebson's a nasty thing*?'

'Listen atom-brain. We do it the other way. How about – Don't stop at lunch time. Teachers unite. One out, all out. Close the school down. How about that?'

Jonah suddenly looked at his friend. 'Do you know. Somewhere behind that solid bone, intelligence glimmers, faintly, but still. It'll make Stebson crawl up the railings.'

'Right on. So we start in Art this afternoon. Special hush

hush project. No need to tell Miss Ainsworth. Only upset her.'

By late afternoon, news of the rival demos had begun to filter through the school. Staff began to have their suspicions, but with pupils being cleared out of the school during lunch break, the intelligence system was not working as it usually did.

'Think they are up to something, Dan?' Baxter asked Hopwood in the staff room.

'They could be, but whatever it is, if it's in their lunch hour I'm not supervising them.'

Stew, Duane and the others got the message that same day. Opinions were divided immediately.

'Well, I reckon Gripper's got a point, what right have the teachers got to close the place down? It's our school as much as theirs.'

'Ho, ho,' replied Stew. 'Since when have you loved this school that much. Or G. Stebson for that matter.'

'That's not the point. It doesn't matter who's doing the demo, it's the principle that counts.'

'Well, I'd sooner drop dead than walk down the road behind Stebson and his apes. As for principle, Stebson's never heard of it. He's out to stir it up, that's all.'

'So what do we do? Everybody else is marching. We can't join in with the second years.'

'No-o. But we could do our own thing.' Stew thought for a moment. 'How about, Fair Deal for Staff and Students: Pay Up and Open Up.'

'Not bad.'

Claire and Suzanne joined the group just as Stew was talking. Claire said: 'Hey, what's all this. Can anybody join in or is it private?'

'Since you ask,' said Duane coldly, 'It is.'

'What's that supposed to mean?' demanded Claire.

'You have your secrets, we have ours.'

'What secrets?' Claire was angry now.

'Don't be so flaming innocent,' said Duane.

'Don't you talk to me like that, Orpington,' Claire turned her back and walked away. Suzanne stared at them.

'Children, children.'

Stew shook his head.

'Who's pressed your button, mate? What was all that for?'

'Oh, forget it,' snapped Duane, and marched out.

Chapter 24

'Something is up,' Dan Hopwood remarked to Miss Lexington as they saw the last customer off the premises at lunch time that Friday.

'How so, Dan?'

'They went so quietly, like lambs. Yet there was a wicked air about them all. We are going to have trouble this lunch time.'

'Are you sure, Dan? It seems to have settled down these past few days. Been quite humdrum.'

He grinned: 'I know. As we used to say, have a look in at 3H, they've been quiet for five minutes, they must be up to something.'

They turned away from the gate and strolled back into the main building. As they entered, McGuffey charged past. Dan called him back.

'What news from the airlines, Mike?'

'What d'you mean, what news?'

Lexington and Hopwood opened their eyes wider. McGuffey's tone was unpleasant to say the least.

'I mean we ought to know soon. We'll have to get a move on if the whole holiday isn't going up the shute.'

'Look, mate,' McGuffey rounded on Hopwood, 'I am doing my best, I can't do any more. There is no more news and to be honest, I couldn't care less.'

'Oh, great,' said Dan, 'that's just the way to go about it.'

McGuffey's lips came together, then he burst out:

'I'll tell you what isn't the way to go about it. And that's organising another flaming out-of-school event just when we're in the middle of an industrial dispute.'

'What event?'

'This one you and the Head dreamed up, this money raising caper. We tell the authorities enough's enough and you go right ahead and do the opposite. And you're supposed to be the union rep.'

Hopwood's voice was level.

'Look, supposing you do your job properly and leave me to do mine.'

There was a silence in the passage, then the staffroom door opened and Terri Mooney and Graham Sutcliffe came out, looking rather strained, as if they too had been having words. They stopped at the sound of Hopwood's voice.

McGuffey spoke. Or rather he shouted.

'As far as this particular job is concerned, this school journey lark, I'm not interested in doing it anyway, good or bad. In fact from now on, I'm finished. Anything bar the bare minimum I do not do.'

He thrust the folder marked *School Journey*, which he was holding, into Hopwood's arms and marched out. The others looked at one another.

'Well, we are in a state,' murmured Sutcliffe.

Miss Mooney came closer to Hopwood. She held out her hand.

'Don't look so glum, Dan. You've done your best. You can't please everyone.'

'That I know,' he answered. 'But neither can I do everything. Who's going to look after the Journey Committee now?'

'That's what I mean,' she said, taking the folder from him. 'I'll do it.'

Behind her Sutcliffe suddenly burst out in exasperation.

'You can't do that. If you take on anything more, you won't know whether you're coming or going.'

'You mind your own business,' responded Miss Mooney tartly. Turning she marched smartly back into the staff room, leaving Hopwood, Lexington and Sutcliffe speechless.

Chapter 25

'Now here's a happy man coming.'

From his seat in the bar of the King's Arms, Paddy Riordan leaned over to nudge Sam Green. They sat with two of their mates from the demolition site across the high road, drinking their post-lunch Guinness. The others turned to look as a lanky, young man, hair untidy, expression grim, marched in through the street door.

'Mr McGuffey!' called Paddy. 'Over here.'

'Come and have one on the National Health,' he added.

'National Health?' asked McGuffey, sitting down nodding to Sam Green and the others.

'Yes, like all Guinness should be,' replied Paddy. 'In fact we are clearing a site for them to build the new Out Patients' Department.'

'Hm, some departments can get money,' grumbled McGuffey.

'Ah, yes,' said Paddy, 'but they've only been waiting seventeen years for this one.' He looked up and grinned at the landlord who approached with a tray full of tankards, fished out two crumpled fivers, handed them over, and turned back to McGuffey.

'You look as though you'd won the pools and forgotten to post the coupon, doesn't he Sam?'

'Ah, he does Paddy. But then the teachers' lot is an unhappy one.'

'True. But your lunch hour should be a doddle these days, with all the boys and girls sent out to play in the shopping centre.'

'If I had my way, I'd close the school down altogether until the public came to its senses,' responded McGuffey.

'But that's what Councillor Doyle and the others were

70

trying to do last year,' said Sam Green, 'and you, and the public objected.'

'That's different.'

'You mean, you're at odds with the public?' asked Paddy.

'Too right, mate.' replied McGuffey.

'Why, then?'

'Because they can't seem to see we have a real grievance.'

'Have you tried to tell them?'

McGuffey shrugged and was about to reply when Sam Green held up his hand.

'What's that, Paddy?'

All stopped their chat and listened. From out in the street came a murmuring roar, like a distant football crowd. The sound came closer. Amid the roar sounded the sharper sound of people chanting.

Paddy hauled up to his feet: 'Let see what's going on.'

Half the men in the bar left their seats and went out into the space in front of the pub. From there they had a clear view of the main road and the side street leading up to Grange Hill school.

'Will you look at that now?' said Paddy.

Chapter 26

From three directions, across the traffic lights, over the zebra crossings, even across the line of traffic, now jammed, hooters and horns going full blast, came three marching columns. Each one had seventy or eighty Grange Hillites, advancing in ragged order four and five abreast.

From one side came Gripper and his crew, with their slogans. From the other side came the second years, with some first years backing them, with Jonah, Zammo, Fay and Annette in the lead.

And hastening at a near trot, to place themselves in the middle ground, came Duane, Stew and their friends together with a mixed bunch of pupils who had arrived late and joined the first crowd that came to hand.

As the three armies came closer, their shouted slogans met in mid air and bounced off one another: Close the School Down, Open the School Up. Up with the Teachers, Down with the Teachers.

'This is democracy gone wild,' said Sam Green.

'It is going to be something quite other very shortly,' replied Paddy, his eyes lighting up at the sight of battle. 'Let's get over there, Sam, before they bust the gates in and the ratepayers get the bill.'

The half dozen, McGuffey in the middle, raced across the road below the milling crowd, ran along the further pavement, turned into the side street and reached the school gates just as the first part of the three demos, which had now merged into one struggling crowd, pressed into the opening. Inside the school gates stood Baxter, Hopwood, Sutcliffe and Mr Thompson, the school caretaker. They stared amazed as McGuffey, Paddy and his mates arrived to station themselves outside.

'Open up the gates,' roared Gripper and his mates.

'Close the school down,' yelled Zammo and his contingent, a little higher up the octave.

'Fair dos for all,' came the cry from the social democrats in the middle.

'Bust the gates open,' shouted one of Gripper's men and their part of the crowd surged forward.

'We'd better get the police,' said Mr Thompson.

'Perish the thought,' replied Paddy, through the gates. 'Why spoil the fun?' He turned to McGuffey. 'It's your turn now.'

McGuffey goggled at him. 'My turn?'

'True lad. Your turn. I mean your chance. Your opportunity. Put your case to the public.'

'What public?'

'Why the public that's closest to you, man. The consumers. Tell it to them. Go on. Get up on the wall.'

'What about?'

'Never mind about them. Up you get and start talking.'

Bewildered, but not unwilling, McGuffey clambered up on the wall and held out his hands for silence. A terrific shout went up, then there was silence. McGuffey began to speak.

'I would like to explain . . .' he began.

Gripper's voice cut across: 'We don't want to know.'

Paddy advanced towards Gripper's group: 'Will you be quiet and listen to the gentleman before I stuff that poster so far up your jumper you'll be wearing it permanently.'

In the silence that followed, McGuffey began to speak again. The crowd drew quietly nearer. Behind the gate, the other teachers began to relax.

'Excuse me,' someone was at Duane's elbow. He turned. A tall, sharply dressed young man, notebook in hand, was there.

'Are you one of the organisers of this happening?'

'Not me, mate,' said Duane, jerking his thumb at Stew. 'Who are you?'

'I'm Jeremy Hart. I'm from the local rag. Now can you tell me who that is speaking?'

73

Chapter 27

Easter holidays came along and, guess what happened, the fine weather vanished like magic and everywhere was grey, cold and miserable. Of course the weather suited the mood of a lot of people.

But then some people are never satisfied.

The news was good. The teachers' pay claim went to arbitration and the Great Lock Out was called off, for the moment.

'What's arbitration?' Zammo asked Jonah. 'It sounds painful.'

'It's quite simple,' Jonah explained. 'When two people fall out, they go to this special geezer. He listens to both sides, then he makes up their minds for them.'

'And everybody's happy.'

'No, nobody's happy, but they have to put up with it.'

'Thanks, Jonah. You've made it clear as mud.'

'Stick with me. There's more, much more.'

So Jonah and Zammo went off on their Easter break. Jonah had more or less decided he didn't mind going on the school journey. And both of them were beginning to look forward to it, getting right away, to a new place where no one knows you and you can get up to all kinds of things.

They spent Easter roaming round the neighbourhood, looking at some of the new spots that Zammo had found while playing follow my leader with Gripper during the lunchtime lock out.

Gripper himself had gone to earth. He and his recruits had disappeared from the landscape. They were a bit disappointed with him. They'd been promised aggro. But they'd only got to march down the road with stupid posters and nearly get their heads busted by a dirty great demolition worker. It had not been one of Gripper's most brilliant terms, and he needed to think things over. It wasn't the way to set up a permanent outfit that would spread alarm and despondency in Grange Hill.

So Gripper had to mark his end of term report, 'Could do better.' And he wasn't speaking to anyone.

Mrs McCluskey wasn't speaking to anyone either. On the Friday when school broke up, she had seen the local newspaper, where Jeremy Hart had done his job on Grange Hill's industrial troubles.

'Teachers with backs to wall as angry pupils storm school,' was his version. He had even worked in Paddy and Sam Green with 'parents join in demo against staff action'.

Together with Jeremy Hart's 'report' went yet another 'more in sorrow than in anger' piece from the editor, saying, '*Still* waiting for the good news from Grange Hill'.

Mr Keating told the head: 'It wasn't quite as he described it.'

'I know,' she answered impatiently. 'But the public doesn't know that. I think I must do something about that local paper after the holiday.'

Just what she would do she didn't say. Instead she packed her bag and went home.

Dan Hopwood and McGuffey went home too. They were still not speaking to each other after their row and McGuffey had pulled right out of the school journey organisation.

Mooney and Sutcliffe went home, but they weren't speaking either. Terri Mooney was going to spend her holiday ringing up airlines and travel agents trying to find cheaper tickets for the school journey. Graham was going to have to spend the holiday looking at his stamp collection.

Pogo wasn't speaking to anyone. He was going to spend his holiday stripped off in the bathroom looking down between his toes at the scales. Every time he climbed on to them, the indicator seemed to go further round. At night he lay in bed and worked out wild schemes for nipping into the gym and school and tampering with the scales there before the big School Journey Event Day.

Annette and Fay weren't speaking, either. Annette was

going to spend a lot of time during the holiday getting ready for the brilliant scheme she had worked out for the Event Day. The fact that people like Claire had muscled in and taken it over didn't seem to worry Annette. She thought the whole thing was a giggle and couldn't see why Fay couldn't share her point of view.

Fay was quite frankly, just disgusted. The whole business was so cosmically stupid she couldn't bear to think about it. So Annette went her way for the holidays and Fay went hers.

Duane and Claire were very much not speaking. At least, when they did speak to one another the results weren't all that encouraging.

As Claire, Suzanne and several other girls left school that day, Duane was waiting for her at the school gate.

She took one look at his face, shrugged and screwed up her lips at her friends and went to one side to have a quiet word with him.

'Look,' he said, 'I'm a bit fed up with all this. Are you coming out tonight, or aren't you? You've been messing about for days now.'

She bit her lip.

'I'm sorry, Duane, but I absolutely can't. We've got this thing to organise. It's going to take a bit of doing, but, look I'll ring you at the weekend.'

'Listen,' he said, controlling his anger, 'can't you at least tell me what you're up to? I've got a right to know.'

'Oh, have you? Well, I can't. It's a secret.'

'You're just making this an excuse to mess me about.'

'Don't be childish,' she burst out. The others who had been watching them, ears flapping like radar dishes, started to giggle.

'Oh, sod off,' he swore.

Turning, he blundered out across the road, narrowly escaping the front bumper of the approaching bus.

Claire, speechless, stared after him. What was she going to do now?

Chapter 28

Duane spent a miserable weekend. Claire didn't ring. But that was hardly to be expected. He wondered whether to ring her, but made up his mind that that was the last thing he would do. He knew he ought really to brush the whole business away. Either it didn't matter and he could just see her again next term as if nothing had happened. Or it did matter, in which case he wouldn't be seeing her next term. Or he'd be seeing her and not talking. That would finish that.

But as it was he couldn't do either. The more he thought about it, the more choked and angry he felt. He had to do something before then. But what? Over and over again he could hear himself saying, I'm not letting her get away with that. What 'that' was he couldn't say.

At the end of the weekend, he'd made up his mind what to do. Well, he didn't really think it out. He just did it, as though someone else were pulling the levers and guiding him. He started to follow Claire around. At first he had to wait a day or two because she didn't seem to be doing anything except shop for her mother. But then one day he struck lucky. He picked her up coming out of their place mid-morning and tailed her down to the Arndale. She was going to that same cafe.

There she teamed up with Suzanne and two other girls and who should they meet but Green, Benny Green again. But this time he had an older bloke with him. Duane had a feeling he knew the bloke's face, but he couldn't say from where. He wasn't a bloke from school. But he was local. He was well known for something, but what Duane couldn't say.

They stayed there for nearly an hour and in the end left all together, joking and laughing. Duane watched them go and kicked the wall in his frustration.

That night he tried to phone her, but all she said was: 'I'll talk to you when you're in a better temper.'

'Who's in a bad temper?' he raged.

'You are.'

He slammed the phone down.

Two days later, Claire set off from home again. This time Sherlock Orpington was close, but not too close behind. If he had any hesitations before about following her, they were gone now.

He followed her round to Tracey's place, then they went on to Suzanne's. Then they picked up Precious Matthews. How many of them were there? He stuck with it. Hey, they were picking up second years as well. What a carry on. He began to get excited.

They caught the bus. He clenched his fists in fury. But no – they were all going inside. He raced for the bus, leapt on the back as the conductor rang off and slipped quickly upstairs. Where were they off to?

The bus trundled along, picking up old age pensioners who seemed to take all day climbing on to the platform, women shopping who had to have a joke with the conductor. Duane sat tense, head down in case anyone came on top.

The bus stopped again. He could hear them suddenly giggling and yakking below. He squinted out of the window. Down below on the pavement the whole gang of them had mustered. They were all carrying travel bags. Where were they going? He stood up then crouched down again. As he raised his head once more they were streaming across the pavement. Duane's eyes opened wide now.

They couldn't be going in there? But they were. The bus was moving again. He flung himself down the stairs again, brushed past the conductor and tumbled on to the pavement. But they had all vanished. They'd gone inside.

Baffled, excited, he wandered along the pavement. Was that what she was up to? Stupid. No wonder she 'couldn't' tell him.

Well, he'd see about that. A sudden idea struck him. He broke into a run down the road. A hundred yards along he turned into a phone box and began to look up the number of the local rag.

Chapter 29

On the Friday before school started again, Mrs McCluskey came back into school. Her plan was to spend a quiet day doing paper work. No one else was there. The building was quiet, only the mice and Mr Thompson scampering about. She looked forward to a solid day's effort. The thought of it was almost enjoyable. She made herself a cup of coffee and sat down, at peace with the world.

The cup was just at her lips when the phone rang. It rang on her extension. So she took a quick mouthful of coffee and lifted the receiver to her ear.

'Am I speaking to Mrs McCluskey?'

The voice exploded in her ear. Whoever it was was either new to the telephone or he was very, very angry. He was yelling. It took a moment to even identify the speaker, or the yeller. The Head tried to stop him in his stride. But it was not easy. Mr Scott, Claire's father, had the bit between his teeth and wasn't stopping for anyone.

'What does the school think it's playing at? I'm withdrawing my daughter. I'll have her educated privately. If this is what comprehensive schooling is about, I don't want to know.'

Mrs McCluskey took a deep breath, transferred the phone from one hand to another, forgot she was holding the cup and shot a stream of coffee over her desk.

'Hell,' she whispered.

'I beg your pardon?' bellowed Mr Scott.

'Nothing Mr Scott.' She tried to take charge. 'Will you kindly tell me exactly what has happened so that I can deal with it. I am sure there is nothing that cannot be sorted out.'

'Nothing?' His voice rose as if there had been an emergency operation. 'If you call this nothing, then I'd like to see something.'

'Please Mr Scott, tell me what has happened.'

'You mean you don't know?' Mr Scott was astounded.

'No.'

'Don't you read the local paper? You ought to. It has a lot about your school and not very appetising either.'

'Mr Scott!' Mrs McCluskey suddenly put on her quarter-deck voice and the voice at the other end quietened.

'I have not yet seen the local newspaper. But I'll get one.'

'Don't you worry, Mrs McCluskey. I have one here. I'll read it to you.'

There was the crackle and rustle of pages turning. The head seized her blotter and began to mop up her desk.

'Grange Hill girls in dressing room caper.'

'I beg your pardon, Mr Scott.'

'That's it – in the dressing rooms at the Rovers football ground. And undressed, too.'

'Mr Scott. I do not believe you. What on earth could they have been doing? What are you talking about?'

'Second, third and fourth year girls, Mrs McCluskey. During these holidays they have been in that soccer club, getting stripped off in the dressing rooms.'

'Oh.' Suddenly light dawned on Mrs McCluskey. She began to chuckle. That was fatal.

'If you think it is a laughing matter, I do not, and neither do the other parents.'

'Have you been in touch with them?'

'I have indeed, and they all feel the same way as I do. It's disgusting.'

'All, Mr Scott?'

'Well, most of them. Two or three couldn't seem to care less, but that's just typical. Anyway, it's got to be stopped.'

Mrs McCluskey put on her soothing voice.

'It's all quite clear now. As you know fifty of our pupils are going on a school journey and – – '

'Well, Claire's not. I can just imagine what they'll get up to.'

'We planned a special Events Day to raise money for the air fare. The soccer players among the party challenged all comers and the girls have obviously formed their own football team. It was their idea but we have always tried to encourage them to take initiative . . .'

'And why weren't we told?'

'I assume the girls wanted to keep it a secret.'

'In view of what's in this newspaper, I'm not surprised.'

'Mr Scott, you should not take everything written in the Press as absolutely true.'

'Are you denying it?'

'I have not yet seen it. When I see it, I shall have a word or two to say to the editor.'

'That's up to you. Now I want that business called off.'

'Mr Scott, that is a large demand. You can of course forbid Claire to take part.'

'I have done.'

'And?'

'She said I was talking like a Victorian grandfather.'

'Oh. Look, Mr Scott. I think the best thing is for you and Mrs Scott, and Claire to come in and see me. Is Monday convenient?'

'I shall make it convenient, Mrs McCluskey,' said Mr Scott, menacingly.

Chapter 30

Monday was a day of high excitement. All through the morning and afternoon the big debate raged, both girls and boys divided among themselves. Comments ranged from 'stupid', to 'great', with brilliantly witty remarks like, 'I wonder what strip they use?'

In Mr Hopwood's form though, another debate was going on. How, demanded Claire furiously, had that rat Jeremy Hart on the local rag, got on to the girl's soccer team?

'Oh, he's around everywhere,' said Stew. 'Someone at the Rovers could have tipped him off for a fiver. Some people do anything for money.'

'Yeah,' muttered Duane looking away. Claire gave him a curious glance. He had been very quiet since they came back. She had not seen him all through the holidays and she had begun to feel sorry they had quarrelled. But right now she had enough troubles without worrying about Duane's feelings.

'What's going to happen now?' demanded Pogo, always glad to see the heat off him and on someone else.

Claire shrugged. 'All the parents are coming in after school. They're going to talk it over in the head's office.'

'Hey, will you be there?'

'Never. We'll have to wait outside like good little girls.'

'Well, good luck, Claire, anyway,' said Stew.

'Yeah,' said Duane in a strangled voice.

So many parents came to see the Head that the meeting had to be shifted to the library. They packed in around the tables and the Head stood in the middle, supported somewhat nervously by Mr Keating. He knew trouble when he saw it.

It was clear from the start that it was going to be a duo act.

The rest of the parents said little or rather Mr Scott gave them little chance to say anything.

'I must emphasise that this soccer team was an initiative by the girls, and not the school. Therefore we cannot simply ban it as Mr Scott suggests. However,' Mrs McCluskey paused and looked round at the parents, 'everyone is at liberty to say whether they would like their daughter to take part in such an activity. In my personal opinion it was an unorthodox, but enterprising idea of the girls. They meant well. Perhaps they should have consulted.'

'Perhaps!' exploded Mr Scott.

'But then they wanted to keep it secret. It is only a pity that the local Press decided to sensationalise the story as part of its campaign against the school.'

Two or three parents nodded. Mr Scott was on his feet again.

'So the school won't ban it.'

Before the Head could answer, a tall, wiry lady rose from the back of the audience. It was Precious Matthews' mother.

'I'd just like to say that not everyone feels like Mr Scott does. I think the local paper story is a load of hot air.' She swung round and looked Mr Scott in the eye. 'If the girls had used the soccer ground to train for a hockey match, what would they have said then? Girls these days expect a lot more freedom than we used to have and I say good luck to them. I,' she emphasised the word, 'am sure my daughter is not up to anything she shouldn't.'

There was an uneasy silence. Then Mr Scott rose.

'Very well then, Mrs McCluskey. I shall withdraw my daughter from this – this business and I shall consider withdrawing her from the school.'

He rose and marched out. Others followed until only three were left. Mrs McCluskey looked at them.

'I'm sorry. Perhaps we can think of something. But at the moment I can't think what.'

Chapter 31

Two days later, Baxter, Hopwood, Miss Mooney and the Head met together in her office. Faces were gloomy.

Baxter spoke: 'I think we have to go ahead with the Events Day, despite all this aggravation over the girls' soccer team. We have all the other things lined up, computer demonstration, Brain of Grange Hill Quiz, circuit running, weight watching. The old boys' soccer team is lined up, and I still have hopes of a parents' team.'

'Not with Mr Scott, eh?' asked Hopwood. But nobody smiled. 'The trouble is,' Miss Mooney pushed back her hair, and pulled papers from the file on the table before her, 'that even if we reach our target, and that's by no means certain, we are still about £15 per head short of the cheapest air fare I can negotiate.'

'Maybe we should fall back on coach transport,' said Mrs McCluskey.

'Oh, dear me no, that would disrupt the holiday programme completely,' said Hopwood, 'now that Rolf has everything fixed up with Frau Schindler, we cannot chop and change. We don't want to offend her. Who knows, if it went well, we might want to go back there in future years.'

'Well, we must decide in the next ten days,' put in Miss Mooney, 'otherwise we won't have any option.'

Baxter shook his head. 'No, as far as the Events Day is concerned, we have to decide right now. It's next Saturday, remember. I want us to go ahead,' he said firmly.

The other three looked at the Head. She tapped the desk. 'If it fails to attract many parents, it could do us actual harm. I'm afraid that there is considerable bad feeling about over this girls' football team. It is amazing how upset people become, but I have to take account of their feelings.'

Hopwood smiled: 'I think that in a week or two's time Mr

Scott will calm down. He has a tendency to fly off the handle. And when he quietens down, so will other people. As for withdrawing Claire from school, he will think better of that, I'm sure. To switch schools now would be a disaster for Claire.'

'If only we were sure he was actually thinking of what is good for Claire,' said Miss Mooney.

'Let us hope Mrs Scott can get to work on him,' said Mrs McCluskey. 'She had nothing to say at the meeting.'

'Can you wonder?' asked Miss Mooney.

The Head changed the subject quickly. 'I must have a little more time to think about this. Can we have a word tomorrow morning, first thing?'

The others nodded, and filed out of the office.

After lunch the Head left her work and went for a brisk walk in the park. Problems always seemed worse when one sat still. Even if no solution was in sight, moving along in the fresh air made her feel better. Her mind working hard, she made several circuits, suddenly realising she had walked three times round the duck pond and the park keeper was eyeing her suspiciously. She looked at her watch. Lunch hour was long past. She had been walking for an hour.

As she came hastily back in her office, her secretary called: 'Someone on the phone. A gentleman. Very urgent. He rang two times when you were out.'

'Indeed?' Not Mr Scott again? She crossed her fingers and picked up the receiver on her desk. No, not Mr Scott, but another, more friendly voice.

'Mrs McCluskey, Hardcastle here.'

She stared blankly at the wall. The way he spoke she ought to know who 'Hardcastle' was, but she didn't.

'My fault really, I suppose.'

'Oh, I'm sorry . . .'

'No reason for you to be. You see it was done as a favour for Benny Green.'

'Benny Green?' Mrs McCluskey shook her head as if that might clear it. 'But he's not with us, these days.'

'I know, Mrs McCluskey. He's with us. He's on the ground staff at the Rovers.'

Mrs McCluskey suddenly saw light at the end of a long tunnel.

'Next year he'll be turning out for our first team. Good lad that, he'll make the top if he shapes.'

'I'm glad.' Mrs McCluskey was baffled again.

'He asked me if this girls' soccer team could use our changing rooms on odd mornings in the Easter break. Very hush hush. I thought it was a lark you know. Until I saw the local rag – that bast – – – I beg your pardon, that man Hart. He's done that kind of hatchet job on me before. I've told him I don't want to see him on the Rovers' ground any more.'

'Hm, but why?'

'Oh yes. This is the point. That Events Day of yours. We want to help. We'll turn out a scratch team for you. Veterans if you like. There's a couple of 'em have played for Spurs, one was capped for England. Known names. We'll play all-comers. And I tell you what, I'll get on to the editor of that rag and tell him to give you a good show this weekend or his Cup Final tickets are up the spout.'

'Well, Mr Hardcastle, I'm overwhelmed.'

'Don't be. You haven't seen us play yet. But look forward to meeting on the day. 'Bye.'

Mrs McCluskey put down the phone. She sat for a while in thought, then suddenly smiled. She had an idea.

Chapter 32

The day of the Events began with miserable, grey weather and flurries of rain. Baxter and other members of the staff first to arrive looked out over the deserted school grounds, then looked at each other.

'We ought to have our heads seen to,' murmured Sutcliffe.

'Too late for that, chum,' answered Baxter. 'In for a penny in for a pound now.'

'Three guesses which it's going to be.'

'Oh come on. They'll turn up. We did have rather a good piece in the local rag yesterday – Rovers help Grange Hill.'

'Bit late in the day, after all the garbage they've turned out.'

'Don't knock it, Graham. Anyway, let's get to work.'

Hopwood arrived, out of breath.

'Sorry, I'm late. Look, the sun's coming out,' he said.

So it was. By 11 o'clock when the day proper began, the wind had chased the last clouds away and the sun was shining strongly. Asphalt in the school yard began to steam and the helpers, staff and pupils began to throw off jackets and roll up sleeves. Before long the day was in full swing.

By noon it was clear that the place was going to be crowded. Parents and former pupils began to arrive in droves. Staff began to look at each other and grin. They could have a success on their hands.

The events started, one surprise after another. To the astonishment of all concerned G. Stebson, who had last been seen catching a crafty drag behind the gym, completed seven circuits of the football pitch and came off the track with hardly a bead of sweat on his brow.

'He's in better condition than you'd think,' muttered Jonah grudgingly.

'Yeah, worse luck,' answered Zammo. 'All goes to show.

We have to keep behind him. No good getting in front.'

The next surprise came when the weigh-in started and Douglas Patterson was not there in the flesh. Not at all. Nowhere to be seen in fact.

But a quick search by Baxter soon winkled out Pogo, crouched down behind the scales in the gym. He was not worshipping them, unfortunately, but trying to doctor them to get rid of seven pounds of excess weight that he hadn't succeeded in losing.

A short sharp interrogation very soon revealed the truth. Baxter glared at the luckless Patterson.

'What are we going to do with you, mate, apart from boil you down and use what's left for some useful purpose?'

'Don't know, sir,' answered Pogo wishing he could literally disappear.

'I know, sir,' said Stew. 'Let's make a virtue out of necessity.'

'A which out of what?' asked Baxter.

'You know, instead of a sponsored slim, let's make the most of what we have – run a Guess His Weight competition.'

Baxter grinned wolfishly.

'Good thinking Robin. Right,' he turned to Pogo. 'Into your sports gear and get round to the hall.'

'The hall?' Pogo's voice dwindled.

'I did say that. This is either public or it isn't. How do the customers guess your weight if they can't see the goods?' He turned to Stew. 'Go and see Mr Thompson. Borrow a trolley and we'll run the scales over there. We could save the day after all.'

But the day was due not only to be saved, but made.

In the afternoon, when the crowds were at their thickest, Hardcastle and his veterans turned out on the football pitch. They wore a motley strip, from almost every known team.

Amid cheers, they took on first the School Journey team, coached to the peak of perfection by Baxter and after twenty minutes play, were lucky to draw one all.

Next they wore the parents' team down to a two nil defeat

and after a quick rest and munch at an orange slice, they destroyed the staff team five one.

It was at this point that Baxter caused his sensation. Taking the loud hailer, he announced, amid silence, the Match of the Day. Hardcastle's veterans would now in their final match meet a Mystery Team, one, he declared, never before seen, or its like in British Soccer.

Hardcastle's men gathered again half joking to one another. The crowd waited. Nothing happened. The fourth years in the crowd began a rhythmic hand clap and a chorus of 'Why are we waiting'.

Suddenly the double doors to the gym went back with a crash and out on to the grass came the Mystery Eleven. At first there was silence again, but then came laughter, quickly followed by clapping and finally cheers.

First on to the field came Annette, doing her captain's bouncing act with the ball, and saluting the crowd as she went. Next came Precious, tall lithe and sporty, Suzanne, awkward looking but defiant. Then as they moved up to the centre line, there was a pause.

'Where's the rest? Typical women! You need eight more for a team!'

'Shut your faces,' responded Suzanne, as on to the field came the rest of the team, one by one. Shouts of recognition came from the touchline.

'Hey, there's Trisha Yates, hey and Cathy Hargreaves, and Susi and Pamela Cartwright. Who's that behind 'em?'

'I don't know. Hey, no! It can't be. It's Precious Matthew's mum.'

'There's Miss Mooney, and Lexi.'

Then, 'Hey, I don't believe it. Look who's there!'

Bringing up the rear, acknowledging the cheers which now reached a crescendo, came Mrs McCluskey.

'Good old Bridget,' yelled an unseen wit.

'Right,' roared Baxter over the loud hailer. 'Settle down. Ten minutes a side. No punching, ear twisting or eye gouging and may the best – persons win.'

Chapter 33

It was a fast and furious match amid a continuous roar from the crowd and in the nineteenth minute, Annette, small, fast and nippy went through a melee in the goal mouth to put the Ladies' XI ahead by the only goal.

The crowd swarmed on to the pitch and surrounded the players as they struggled back to the gym with the help of the staff. As Mrs McCluskey reached the steps, she was stopped by the local press photographer demanding a picture with Mr Hardcastle. She frowned for a moment, then agreed.

As they posed arms round shoulders, someone came up on her left and spoke.

'Congratulations, Mrs McCluskey.'

She turned and stared at the young man with the smooth voice.

'I'm Jeremy Hart, of the Gazette.'

She turned away. 'I'm not sure I want to talk to you Mr Hart.'

'Oh dear. I thought I might get a vote of thanks.'

'Indeed, and why?'

'I doubt very much if these crowds would have been here today if it hadn't been for my original story.'

Words failed her. She glared and moved on into the gym.

Later that afternoon when the closing ceremony was over and it was clear that the school journey target had been smashed, Dan Hopwood stopped the Head on her way down the hall.

'Congratulations,' he said.

She grinned: 'Thank you. I felt a bit of a fool at one point, but then,' she looked closely at him, 'it did me good to get out of my bunker for a bit.'

He stared, then went slightly red. She laughed.

'Well it was a long shot. But it was you I overheard that day when the withdrawal of goodwill started?'

He grinned now. 'Yes. One should never talk under open windows in a school.' Then he added: 'There's more good news. I've made contact with a school party flying to Munich. Nearly the same dates as ourselves. If we can adjust one day, we can travel together, that puts us over a hundred bodies and we get a fifteen per cent discount.'

'What astonishing luck,' she said.

'Well no, actually, management. I've been asking around and met this colleague last night.'

'Oh, where?'

'At a Union conference.'

Chapter 34

If the Events Day was a success, then the Journey Disco at the school which came at the end of term was sensational.

All the notables, past and present, were there, even T. Jenkins made an appearance escorting Pamela Cartwright and big Alan came along with Susi.

More surprises. Mr and Mrs Scott turned up with Claire, and were seen to be smiling. Claire was going on the school journey after all.

Duane keeping quiet and still looking guilty got to dance with Claire. With any luck, he thought, she would never find out who it was who had passed the bubble to Jeremy Hart. He'd have to crawl a bit for a while until it all blew over. Claire, relieved that the unpleasant part of the business was over, danced with Duane. But she found his behaviour a bit funny. There was something wrong. She'd have to wheedle it out of him sometime.

Fay danced with Rolf, but found she was in competition with Miss Lexington. Annette danced with everyone who came within reach irrespective of age, rank or sex. She was over the moon now that her soccer team idea had come off. Now, she thought, we can start a regular soccer team for girls at school – or better still, she chuckled to herself, a mixed team. If the boys could stand it.

Pogo didn't dance but sat modestly at the side nibbling now and then at a sausage roll. After an afternoon spent exposed by the side of the scales in the school hall, he was beginning to feel just a bit embarrassed about the weight question.

And Suzanne? She danced not once, or even twice, but several times with Dan Hopwood. One way and another he had gone up several notches in her estimation. He had promised to find a way round the money question for the school journey without making her feel like a beggar with a tin cup, and he had done it. Well they'd all done it.

They'd become closer too. It was easier to get on and talk with him, as though they were the same age – almost. She grinned at him. He grinned back and she swung round to the music, round and round.

When she swung back again, he was lined up with Miss Mooney and she was landed with Mr Sutcliffe. She grinned at him too. She was ready to be really decent to everybody tonight. But he didn't grin back. He looked gloomy.

The night went on. The aged and the weaklings slowly departed and the pace got faster and faster. Finally, when time was beginning to run out, came a mini disaster. Or a maxi disaster according to how you look at it.

Suzanne determined to dance with Mr Hopwood as the evening closed, worked, or fought her way through the scrum under the revolving lights. She reached his side and called his name but amid the din of music, chat, laughter and shrieking, he didn't seem to hear her. She caught his hand and he swung round.

Too far. With a lurch he lost balance, slid down and shot forward, one leg doubled under him.

For a moment there was pandemonium. The music stopped and Baxter and Lexington struggled through the crowd to reach Hopwood who was levering himself off the floor. His face seemed to go green with the effort. Baxter knelt down.

'Well mate. Casualty Department for you as soon as we can make it.'

Chapter 35

Suzanne walked slowly down the corridor of the hospital carrying a bunch of flowers. She wondered whether that was right or not. Usually you bought flowers when people had rolled up. But chocolates didn't seem right. She felt so stupid she didn't know where to put herself, and she'd only got this far by a tremendous effort of will power.

The nurse showed her into the ward and smiled encouragingly. 'I'm sure your father will be all right. He'll be out of here in a fortnight.' She patted Suzanne's shoulder. 'A broken leg's nothing these days.'

When she reached the bed side she was suddenly annoyed to see that Mr Hopwood wasn't by himself. Sitting next to the bed was McGuffey. He looked embarrassed, as well, for some reason.

Hopwood's smile put her at her ease. They chatted about the Events Day, the disco, as if it had just happened, as though she hadn't crippled him. He looked up shrewdly at her.

'Don't worry about it. It could happen to anybody.' He turned the conversation. 'Anyway, you'll soon be off on the Journey. It'll be great. I'm only sorry I won't be there.'

She looked down.

'I'm not going.'

'What's that?'

'I'm not going. I feel so stupid. It's my fault.'

He frowned at her.

'Hey, you're going and no messing. If I have to get up and kick you on to the plane with my bad leg.' Then he smiled. 'Look I'm relying on you.'

'What for?'

'Who else is going to write to me and tell me what they all get up to?'

She looked away.

'I mean it,' he went on. 'I shall be out of action for a month. I'm counting on you for reading matter.'

Suddenly she felt pleased, but embarrassed. She got up, grinned at him and then at McGuffey.

'OK. Get well soon.'

'Right on, Suzanne. And look after yourself.'

When she had gone, Hopwood turned to McGuffey.

'Look mate, I feel like one of those little dying boys in the old Victorian melodramas. But I've got to say the same thing to you.'

'What's that Dan?'

'I mean, you have to go.'

'What, on the school journey. Never, mate. I pulled out at the crucial moment. I'd feel a bit of a berk going back in now.'

'Forget it, Mike. Look you've got to go, because they'll need you to make up the numbers, ballast on the plane or something.'

McGuffey got up.

'OK, Oliver Twist. You can die happy. I'll go. The Alps could be refreshing.'

Dear Mr Hopwood

We're off. More or less. We took off on time. No strikes, no power cuts, no hi-jacks (yet) no earthquakes. Weather fairish. But what do you care, lying there with your feet up (sorry foot up) and that blonde nurse peeling a grape?

If this letter sounds crazy you can put it down to lack of oxygen. We're cruising at 28,000 feet above Belgium. Or else you can put it down to jet lag. We've crossed the time zone. We're now an hour ahead of ourselves. And some of us haven't caught up with ourselves yet.

Rolf explained it all to me, in his inn–inimi – his nice way. We are on GMT plus one and the rest of Europe more or less is on GMT plus 2. I asked him why the rest of Europe had to be so stupid and he said that where we are going it sometimes seems to be the other way round. No comment.

What else? The usual hassle. Two people arrived late. One didn't turn up at all. One was in the loo when the rest of us were going through the departure gate. One got mixed up with a party of Venezuelan nuns and nearly ended up playing the maracas in a convent in Caracas.

One got missed off the party passport list and was nearly taken away by MI5 at the airport. One forgot his Austrian-type identity card. Three were air sick. One would have been sea sick if Mr Sutcliffe had had his way over the channel.

Tonight when we arrive we get our first instalment of spending money, fifty Austrian schillings (they can't even spell properly). Rolf tells me it is about 3p to the schilling.

He says there's a lot of difference between Germans and Austrians. I'll wait and see. At the moment they're all the same to me. Still they can't all be British.

Hey, we're going down now, through the clouds, they look like pink candy floss where the sun's shining. The sun? Yes, down there in Munich they seem to be having a heatwave. Did I pack my bikini along with my boots? More later.

Suzanne

Chapter 36

Blinding sun and blue skies took them unawares at Munich airport. The Grange Hillites collected their luggage and staggered out on the hot concrete where two coaches waited for them. The first driver, lean and grey-haired, came to meet them.

'This is Herr Rothkopf,' said Rolf.

'Where's his shorts and braces?' whispered Annette.

'Herr Rothkopf runs the coach service in Ellertal. He is also Burgermeister in Hochwald.'

'That could be painful. What's Burgermeister?' muttered Jonah.

'Mayor,' added Rolf.

'Hey great. But where's his chain?'

'All right, you lot. Let's have a bit less of the wit, and get your gear on board,' ordered Baxter.

They clambered into the coach.

'Bit small, isn't it?'

'Got to be to get round all those corners.'

'I see no corners.'

'You will, you will.'

And they did. The coaches rolled out on to the approach road and ten minutes later were purling down the autobahn while around them great stretches of forest unfolded green to the skyline. Above them in the distance showed the first mountains.

'Hey they look about ten thousand feet high.'

Rolf smiled: 'Those are foothills,' he remarked, 'about 1200 metres.'

In front Herr Rothkopf began to feed cassettes into the player on his dashboard. The coach resounded. The Grange Hillites picked up the tune and began to roar out, 'Holla hee, holla ho'. But after the first hour, when the frontier had been passed and they were moving into the broad green reaches of the Inn valley in Austria, they had fallen silent. Even conversation ceased.

But the music went on remorselessly as the driver proceeded to feed in folk songs from different regions. 'We have different yodels from every valley,' he announced cheerfully.

'How many valleys are there?' whispered Fay to Rolf.

'I have never counted,' he grinned. 'But there are seventy-four regions.'

'Oh no!'

The road began to climb. On either side the mountains in their greens, browns and distant blue-grey and whites began to close in.

'How high are we now?'

'This is only a valley. We're barely 1,700 feet above sea level.'

'This place Ellertal, where we're going. Is that high up?'

'The valley,' said Rolf, enjoying the effect he was creating, 'is just a little higher than Snowdon.'

'I don't believe you. It can't be!' Fay's eyes became round.

'As the Red Queen said, in *Alice Through the Looking Glass*,' returned Rolf, 'in the Tyrol, they have mountains that would make your hills look like valleys.'

'Hey, how do you know *Alice Through the Looking Glass*?' asked Annette. 'That's English.'

Rolf grinned and said nothing.

'What do they do up here?' demanded Zammo, 'I mean apart from yodel and milk chocolate?'

'Well,' said Rolf, 'to be honest, agriculture isn't where they get most of their money from. It used to be salt and silver mining.'

'Get away.'

'Now it's forestry, salt mining and manufacturing.'

The coaches were swinging their way through a larger town now, factory chimneys, elevators, kilns suddenly dominated the skyline.

'Well, we could have stayed home for that, couldn't we.'

'Just wait. You'll see, now we really go into the mountains.'

The coaches swung to the right, to the left and right again, tumbling the Grange Hillites across their seats. The road became narrower, trees closed in around it and at corners, between clumps of bushes and branches they began to get glimpses of the way they had come winding down into the valley.

'Hey look at that: it's miles down.'

'I don't want to look at that.'

As they climbed the air cooled. The clouds which had built up on the horizon as they drove from the airport now moved across the sun. And the rain began, at first a drizzle, then as the wind freshened, gusts throwing bursts of hail against the windows. Within a quarter of an hour all visibility had vanished in rain and mist and the party sat silent while in front of them Herr Rothkopf drove steadily on, eyes fixed on the moving triangle of vision cleared by the windscreen wiper. He swung the bus expertly to and fro and there were no more yodelling cassettes. Slowly the party began to realise they were tired. Some tried to sleep, leaning their heads on each others shoulders. One or two began to wish they hadn't come.

'What a carve up. It was sunshine in Munich. I want my money back,' grumbled one.

'Right mate,' said Baxter genially. 'Next bit of flat ground, you can have it and walk back.'

Miserable silence again, as the evening brought dusk to add to the clouds. They passed through villages, the houses looming through the mist. First one, then another, the winding road, the uphill climb the grinding change of gears began to get on the travellers' nerves.

Suddenly Herr Rothkopf pulled off the road into a broad, empty space. Through the mist they could see a black belt of forest, closer to them a blank wall of brown-grey rock, glistening with rain. He turned round.

'Here, we get off. The coach cannot go further.'

Chapter 37

Tired and cramped, the Grange Hillites staggered from the bus and gathered grumpily round their teachers. The rain had stopped, the mist hung down in great grey swathes, the ground under their lightly-shod feet was a mixture of stone and grey mud.

'Yeuch,' said Suzanne. 'Wait till I see Hopwood. He persuaded me to go on this caper.'

'We could always lynch Rolf,' muttered Duane. 'It was his brilliant suggestion.'

'You could,' said Sutcliffe looming behind them. 'Now make sure you have all your gear from the bus.'

'Why what's going to happen?'

'You're going to walk, that's what. You came for a walking holiday, didn't you?'

'He's kidding.'

'He's not, are you sir? But where?'

'Rolf says it's up there,' said Sutcliffe pointing into the mist.

'Yeah, and so's Dracula.'

At that moment there was a howling bark from the heights above them. Everyone was suddenly silent.

Then: 'What's that, a wolf?' asked a first year, thinking how far he was from his mother.

'Get off. They died out years ago.'

The barking came nearer and behind it came the scraping sound of paws and claws on rock. And,

'Look at that,' yammered Pogo.

Out of the mist, heading straight for them, came a massive, sharp-jawed creature, fur glistening with wet. It paused a few yards away, then began to circle them, coming closer.

'Hey, clear off,' said Claire nervously.

'He doesn't understand,' said Pogo contemptuously. 'I

know what they say in the films: He pointed at the dog and yelled: Raus – hund!'

The great creature sprang, placed two huge paws on Pogo's shoulders backed him up against the coach and began carefully to lick his face.

'Oh Douglas, he likes you,' said Claire.

'Yeah, for supper,' added Duane.

A shrill whistle sounded from above. The great dog vanished as soon as it had appeared. From the mist now came the sound of a tractor, and above it the sound of a girl's voice singing.

'More local yodels,' said Stew.

'Hey, it's not. She's singing in English.' The sound came closer.

'The hills are a-crawl, with the English tourists,

With knobbly knees and a la, la la . . .'

Round into the space where they stood swung a farm tractor towing a huge trailer. At the wheel was a tall young man with a blond beard. 'He's terrific. Hey look at that – shorts and braces.'

'That's Friedl, our guide,' announced Rolf. Friedl rose in the tractor seat and waved his hand. 'All luggage on the trailer, please.'

Behind Friedl, in check shirt and jeans, her hair plaited round her head stood a fourteen-year old girl, grinning impudently.

'That is Heidi,' announced Rolf.

'Well, she can get off back to Hollywood,' muttered Pogo, then his voice died, as the great dog suddenly appeared and began to move around them.

'Don't be afraid,' said Heidi, 'that is only Pia. She just wants to smell you all.'

'It would be a woman, wouldn't it,' muttered Pogo.

Friedl called: 'Our farmhouse is only five minutes walk up the road. Please go ahead. We will bring the luggage. Supper is ready. He turned to the staff: 'Frau Schindler apologises for not being here. She is seeing to repair work on the summer pasture farm.'

'I can just picture her,' murmured Baxter, 'like a Russian tractor driver.'

Rolf smiled.

It was half past ten. The younger Grange Hillites, full of noodle soup, smoked pork and sweet pancakes, had been led through into their quarters in the old riding stable beyond the main farmhouse. Whether they were sleeping on straw or not, they barely noticed. They fell into bed and inside twenty minutes the hills were a ring with the sound of snoring.

Staff and helpers were sitting round the cleared table, drinking coffee when Friedl came into the dining room again.

'Frau Schindler invites you to come next door and take a schnapps. We can discuss tomorrow's programme, if you like.'

Eyeing one another, they filed through into the dark wood panelled room with its tiled stove and the ribboned cow bells on the walls, sat down in comfortable chairs while Friedl served their drinks. A door opened and a woman, dressed in white, slim and sunburned, her light brown hair streaked with grey, entered.

'Welcome to Schindlerhof,' she said.

Baxter sat back, nursing his glass, beamed at Frau Schindler and thought to himself.

'Well this beats fishing.'

Chapter 38

Next morning the Grange Hillites woke in a new world. The rain clouds had blown away, the sun shone. A light breeze brought the scent of flowers and hay. They crowded out on to the timber verandah and stared. Across the tree shaded farm yard with its carved trough and strange twisted wooden water spout lay meadows cropped like bowling greens, hay drying golden on wooden racks, more clumps of trees and hills, higher and higher reaching up to a savage wall of jagged red peaks.

Heidi, now in flowered blouse and skirt, joined them.

'Hey what's that?' demanded Pogo pointing.

'That is the Wilder Kaiser.'

'What was he wild about?' asked Duane.

She shook her head. 'The English are always the same, always the same silly jokes.' She turned and went in doors.

'You know what their trouble is,' said Duane, 'no sense of humour.'

'I don't know,' said Stew, 'I thought she was laughing at us last night.'

'I expect,' said Claire, 'she was trying to tell you something and she didn't like stupid comments.'

'Yeah,' said Suzanne, 'it's the story of our lives . . .'

The lads looked at each other. More people crowded out on to the verandah.

'Anyone know where we're going?' asked someone, to be met with shakes of the head.

'Who cares? It's going to be great. Look at the sun.'

'Just look at those houses. All those flowers.'

'Yeah, old Rothkopf even had flowers on the dashboard.'

'And look at those fantastic paintings on the walls.'

'Bet they only do that for the tourists.'

'Hey shut up, if Heidi hears you she'll set Pia on you.'

'Who's Pia?'

'The dog, stupid.'

'That's not a dog. It's a werewolf.'

'She's lovely. She was lying on the stairs when I came down this morning.'

'Yeah, digesting the last English tourist she ate.'

'Ha ha. No, she let me scratch her tum.'

'I wouldn't.'

'Who's offering?'

Zammo who had wandered to the edge of the farmyard suddenly turned round, choking with laughter and pointing.

'Look, over there.'

Across the winding road beyond the farm yard, lay another farm, its timber balconies festooned with red flowers. Below, some twenty lads, all in green shirts and brown leather shorts were assembling.

'Who's that lot?'

'That's a German school.'

'Surprise, surprise. Hey look at 'em. They're going in twos doing follow me leader.'

The Grange Hillites swarmed to the top of the slope and looked down as the German pupils, lads in their early teens, marched past, flanked by their teachers, all in check shirt and shorts. The temptation was too great.

'By the right,' yelled Zammo, and the others took up the chorus. 'Left right, left right. Get in step there. Vee will do the marching.'

The Germans ignored them and marched on heading for the chairlift, where the cable was already in motion, hoisting the chairs up the slope to vanish in the pine woods.

'Catch me doing that kind of caper,' said Duane.

'Right, you lot,' roared Baxter, coming on to the verandah.

'Get your walking shoes on and get lined up. Herr Schindler has a word or two to say to you.'

Friedl appeared in the doorway. 'Today, we shall have a nice easy walk. Not too much up, not too much down. Just to break you in.'

'Remember, his Dad was a horse trainer,' said someone quietly.

Friedl went on: 'One or two simple rules. When we are on the roads, please walk in pairs. When we are on the paths, please go singly. Please do not take short cuts through the meadows, every bit of grass and hay is precious for us, please do not pick the flowers, they are very precious too.'

'Flipping police state,' muttered Duane. Rolf just in front of him turned and frowned. Friedl continued.

'When we walk, please keep behind me. If you get lost when you are behind me that is my fault. If you get lost in front of me, that is your fault. Watch for the markers on stones and stumps, some are red, some red and blue. If you see them, you cannot miss the way.'

And so they set out, down the winding road to join the small river that rushed down into the valley. It was, as Friedl said, an easy walk, for the first day. It was neither very much up, nor very much down. It wandered along by the water, with the rock wall of the mountain rising up alongside of them, and trees taking away the heat of the sun. But there was rather a lot of it. The track did go on and on and when noon had passed, some little feet were rather overheated.

'How much further?' demanded Pogo, surly as he mopped sweat from his neck for the thousandth time.

'Not much further,' responded Friedl and marched on ahead whistling.

'I could get to hate that man,' said Duane.

'I could hate everybody who thought of this idea,' added Tracey, stopping to fish a stone from the side of her shoe.

At last they rested on the brow of a broad sweeping valley and ate packed lunches. 'Please don't throw away your sandwich wrappers,' called Friedl.

They barely seemed to have rested, when the relentless guide had them on their feet. 'It is important not to let the muscles get too stiff on the first day.'

'There won't be a second day,' grunted Zammo. 'I'm going to strangle him.'

'You and whose army,' said Annette. 'He could eat you for breakfast.'

'If the dog doesn't,' added Jonah.

As the afternoon came slowly to an end, they struggled painfully back to Hochwald. The setting sun shone in their faces as they came up the sloping track from the village. Just as they neared Schindlerhof again, they became aware of the mocking voices above them.

'Left right – get your heads up. Let's see you move.'

Baffled, then furious, the Grange Hillites looked up to the balcony of the Becker Farm just above them. Relaxed and in singlets and jeans, or stripped to the waist and lounging on the steps, the German lads pointed and jeered, adding comments that sounded very witty but weren't understandable. As the party reached the Schindler farm verandah and collapsed in small heaps all over the farmyard, Duane turned and glared back at the mocking Germans.

'We're going to have trouble with that mob, I can see,' he said.

'Boots and shoes off on the verandah, please,' called Heidi, who appeared on the steps. 'Supper is at seven.' She looked at Zammo who was marching past her. 'Please don't go inside in your outside shoes.'

'Please shut up,' returned Zammo, mimicking her English and marched past her.

There was a growling sound from inside the farmhouse entrance. Zammo, with the Alsatian's teeth gripping his belt, suddenly reappeared moving rapidly backwards on to the verandah again.

'Hey knock it off, Frankenstein,' he yelled. Heidi grinned.

'You English, have no sense of humour,' she said.

Dear Mr Hopwood

Day Number Three. The weather is lovely. We are settling in. That means fifteen people have blisters, and a dozen have sunburn on their shoulder blades and other parts I can't mention. Guess who's one of them (Ouch). Yes, sunburn. There's a municipal swimming pool and though you can't play ball games in the water, can't play transistors, can't smoke, and can't eat your salami sandwiches and can't talk above a whisper, you can lie and sunbathe, which, after you've marched up and down every spare Alp in the area is very, very soothing.

The country's gorgeous, I have to admit. Just like the post-cards. You expect to see Julie Andrews and a cart-load of nuns come galloping over the meadows. The people – well, I must confess to being a bit surprised. I expected them all to be fat and jolly. But they're all lean and a bit reserved. It's all that rushing up and down the hills. The women work just like the men. I saw Frau Schindler out with a scythe cutting grass the other day. And they all get dressed up in these waistcoats and plus fours and dirndl skirts and walk up and down in their spare time. I thought they did it just for the tourists, but now I'm not sure.

Friedl, the son, and our guide, is super-great. You should see Lexi and Mooney pushing each other aside to sit next to him. Sooty Sutcliffe ought to get very annoyed, but I think he has his eye on Frau Schindler. Meanwhile, on the balcony where Jenkins and Humphreys have rooms next to Cartwright and MacMahon there is much coming and going when sun sets – and much giggling and rushing to and fro in the showers. Personally I think it's all show. I don't think Jenkins is getting anywhere. Cartwright has it all under control. And as far as Humphreys is concerned it's 'down Fido'.

One person *everyone* has their eyes on however, is Erda. She helps in the kitchen, etc. She is a knock-out – so the blokes think, anyway.

The youngest Schindler is Heidi (yes, Heidi!). She is fourteen, very active, very smart, and between you and me, a bit of a pain. She thinks she speaks English better than we do. She's probably right, but still.

Who else is there? Well, at the next farm is a group of lads from a German school. To be honest, they are beginning to get up the noses of one or two of our people. Particularly when they shout rudies we don't even understand.

Stick around. You're not going anywhere are you?

Suzanne.

Suzanne looked at her letter. On impulse she crossed out 'Mr Hopwood' and wrote 'Dan' and put 'love' at the end. Then she crossed that out and swore to herself. She read through the letter once more and suddenly felt embarrassed. She folded it, sealed it in an envelope and put it away in her writing pad. She'd see about posting it later.

Chapter 39

'Oh no,' grumbled Pogo as they assembled on the verandah next day. 'She's not coming, is she?'

Heidi who was sitting, dressed in hiking gear on the rail throwing a ball to Pia the Alsatian, turned at his voice. She had sharp ears. She grinned.

'Of course I am coming. I don't want to miss this.'

'Miss what?'

'Today, we go up on the chair lift, and then up a real mountain.'

'Real mountain?' Pogo stared. 'What are all those flaming things we've been going up yesterday and the day before?'

'Those are – hills. This one is – a mountain.'

Half an hour later, they were soaring up the mountainside seated two by two in the hoist. Some clutched the metal safety rail till their hands hurt. Others waved their arms, pointed and dangled their legs nonchalantly as the chairs rode higher and higher over the pine woods. Soon they were clear of the tree line and into cold and misty air. Now they began to shiver and some of the heroes began to clutch the safety rail. But as they came to ground at the top, the mist was clearing and above them they saw yet another peak, bare and dark in the morning sun. Below them Hochwald had vanished in the white mist clouds.

'Hey that must be ten thousand feet at least,' gasped Zammo.

Big Friedl grinned: 'Six and a half thousand, in fact.'

'Hey,' said Pogo, 'we're not going up *there*, are we?'

Friedl looked at him sharply. 'We are but not you.'

'Why?'

Friedl pointed. 'You have not got your boots.'

There was an immediate shout from the others, half of them jeering at Pogo, half of them protesting. But Friedl

110

shook his head. Baxter came forward: 'Down you go, Patterson.'

'Wait a moment.' Heidi came forward. 'I have a spare pair.'

'They won't fit,' protested Pogo.

Heidi smiled sweetly at him. 'They will. I am sure.'

'Hey, Pogo,' laughed Stew, 'she's been sizing you up.'

'No accounting for taste,' said Suzanne.

And Heidi was right. To Pogo's embarrassment, the boots fitted and soon the whole party was on the march.

Today Friedl seemed to have decided the easy bit was over and he led a smart pace. For nearly three hours, the path zig zagged up through bushes, across bare gullies, round boulders, over streams, along lines of stepping stones set in bogs which sucked in the unwary feet over the ankles. Then finally he led the now footsore, breathless sweating and near mutinous party up the final slope where on a bare crest stood a stone plinth with flag pole and a small timber shrine with crucifix, and the inevitable bunches of flowers.

Friedl turned to his exhausted followers.

'Congratulations. Your first peak.'

'What d'you mean first?' they demanded.

Friedl pulled off his rucksack and produced from it a bunch of small cards which he handed round. 'This is your Wanderkarte. It has seven spaces for seven gipfels, or peaks. When you have climbed all seven, this entitles you to your wandernadel, your badge. At home you can show your friends.'

'My friends'll think I'm crazy,' muttered Jonah.

'Hey no, it's not so stupid,' said Zammo. 'But,' he asked Friedl, 'how do they know you've really climbed the lot?'

Friedl turned to the base of the flagstaff, opened a small door and produced a small rubber stamp on the end of a cord. There was a groan from the party.

'Step up please. I'm sorry there's no pad. We shall have to breathe on it.'

'What with?' demanded Claire.

The climb down took a different route and, though less

111

tiring, was hard on feet and ankles But just as the party had begun to grumble again, Friedl led them over a small wooded ridge, round a bend in the hill and in front of them like magic was a small cafe, where plump middle aged tourists sat placidly drinking coffee in the sun.

Over the flower decked balcony where swallows flitted to and fro was a large notice: Jausenstation.

'What's that mean?' they demanded of Heidi.

'Er – relaxing, rest – station.'

'I see what you mean,' said Stew, as he dropped his rucksack and sank on to a nearby chair.

By the time they reached Hochwald again, the Grange Hillites were firmly divided into two parties, pro-gipfel and anti-gipfel.

'You won't get me dead up one of those again,' muttered Pogo.

But after supper most of them crowded out into the farm yard as if they had never been up a mountain. A ball appeared from somewhere and in ten minutes a mad football game had developed across the yard, up the road, back into the home meadow and up and down the verandah.

Annette, Claire and Precious joined in with the lads, kicking, tackling and pushing and shoving. Suddenly from across the yard they heard ironic laughter and cheering. Lined up on the road were a dozen lads from the German School.

'Girls playing football,' they crowed, pushing one another in their excitement. Duane who was nearest, turned and told the spectators to go forth and multiply.

There was an immediate silence, then one replied: 'Temper, temper.'

Duane, face angry and dark, made a move towards the Germans, but Claire caught his sleeve.

'Don't be so childish. It's only a joke,' she said.

The game died away and people began to drift inside.

Chapter 40

Next day Friedl changed his tactics. He took the party on a gentlish six mile hike up winding roads and paths through woods full of flowers and finally on to a broader way leading through high meadows.

Towards noon, he called a halt at a large cafe with a broad garden full of umbrella shaded tables above a tumbling stream.

'Now,' said he. 'The gipfel party can follow me to our next peak. And the anti-gipfel party can stay here in comfort and eat apfel strudl and drink coffee and coke, until we come back in two hours time.'

'You'll never get up there in two hours,' declared Pogo.

Friedl grinned: 'Oh yes. Today we shall really walk.'

In the end twenty staff and pupils took off behind Friedl, and the rest stayed at the cafe. At first it was pleasant to idle in the sun, eating and drinking, but before the first hour had gone by some people had begun to be restless.

'Bit boring, really,' said Claire.

'Oh, I don't know,' answered Suzanne. She fished out her writing pad and pen. She had already written two letters to Mr Hopwood, giving him all the details of the holiday so far. But she hadn't yet been able to bring herself to post them. They were sealed and unstamped and tucked away inside the pad.

Pogo yawned: 'Wish I'd stayed back at the farm. We could have gone down the village.'

'You're just thinking of one of those ice-creams. What do they call them – chocolate bombs or something?'

'No he's not, he wants to be with Heidi.'

'What,' yelled Pogo in fury, 'fish face? Not likely. Anyway,' he added, 'she's up at the alm.'

'The what?'

'The summer pasture, you ignorant pig.'

'Anyway,' said Pogo heaving himself up and wandering towards the cafe entrance. I'm going back.'

'You can't. It'll take hours and you don't know the way.'

'Get off. It's dead easy. Look,' he pointed out over the meadow. 'See that little hill, shaped like a dog's head? Well Hochwald's just the other side of it. He just brought us the long way round. It's not more than three miles at the most. See, there's a trail leading right up over it.'

'Hey, he's right, you know. Shall we go? That lot could be up the gipfel for hours.'

'What about – – '

'Oh, it's only Mooney and Sutcliffe and they're busy being nice to each other for a change.'

'OK. But not so much noise.'

A group of six, led by Pogo, slipped out of the cafe yard and walked smartly down the narrow track which led through the meadow. Before too long a fold in the ground hid the cafe from sight.

'See, dead easy. You've just got to follow your nose,' said Pogo. 'Look, it's just through this little wood, then up the slope and we're there.'

They pressed on. But the wood somehow seemed bigger, longer and thicker. The path petered out and they struggled through thickets and splashed to their ankles in a boggy stream. They picked up another path. It wound upwards, and after twenty minutes hard slog, they found themselves clear of the trees and out in open moorland.

'Right,' said the leader, 'it's over that brow.'

But it wasn't. Over the brow, stretched more moorland and woods, but no sign of Hochwald with its welcoming pointed roofs.

'Hey we're lost. I can't even see that cafe now.'

'No we're not. We can't be. I worked it out by the sun. Hochwald's over there.'

'What, through that wood?'

The second wood was thicker than the first, and here there was no path at all.

'I reckon we ought to go back.'

'Like which way, stupid.'

'I wish I'd never come. It's Pogo's fault. He knew the flipping way, didn't he?'

'Will you shut up.'

They bumped into one another and stopped, surveying their muddied boots and stockings, their scratched and bleeding legs.

'I thought these paths were marked with blue and red thingies.'

'No path, no thingies.'

'Great.'

'Hey, what's that?'

'What's what?'

'That sound in the bushes. Over there. There's something moving about.'

'Well if it's someone we can ask the way.'

'Not someone. Something. It's an animal. And big too.'

They strained their ears. The rustling, crashing and snapping of twigs came nearer. They grabbed one another and drew in closer.

'It could be a cow.'

'What in the middle of this . . .'

'Or a wolf.'

'Get off. They're all in zoos.'

'How d'you know? You've never been here before.'

'No, and I'm not coming again. I'll strangle Pogo when we get back.'

'Why wait?'

The bushes in front of them suddenly parted. They turned to run in all directions as a huge shape leapt into the tiny clearing. Then Pogo laughed. His voice squeaked.

'Look, it's Pia.'

The huge dog came forward, trotted round them, sniffed at each one and then turned and made off again.

'Hey, let's follow her.'

'What did I tell you? We're right on top of Hochwald.'

115

They plunged on through the bushes behind the bounding dog and soon burst into the open. But they were nowhere in sight of Hochwald. In front of them was more open ground, rough pasture with cows grazing, the bells clanking lazily as they walked. The dog had vanished.

But in front of them, beyond the herd were two low stone buildings. And from them came a familiar sound of someone singing.

'Oh the hills are awash,

With a melting Pogo.'

They ran across the pasture, rounded the corner of the farm buildings, and there at an open window appeared the sunburned face of Heidi. She grinned.

'I saw you through my field glasses. Just where did you think you were going?'

'Oh, Pogo was leading us back to Hochwald.'

'Well, you were doing very well, but you were going in the wrong direction. Anyone like a coke?'

Dear Dan,

Well now, what's new. Last night we all sat on the verandah and listened to two blokes playing the horn and the euphonium on a hill across the way. At first our mob were falling about. But after a bit it gets to you. Makes you want to cry – makes you feel all lovely and miserable.

But surprise. Nobody's homesick any more. Half are running madly up and down mountains trying to win their gipfel badge. The other half are stuffing themselves madly with apple strudl and ice cream. Ice cream here is a meal in itself. And everyone's madly learning useless words in Austrian, I mean German. Knodel is noodle, koch is cook, but gasse means street (!); leber means liver; kissen means cushion; but kussen means kiss, which could get you into trouble. And we all know what yodel is. You can't get away from it.

Now what are we all up to. Mooney still seems to be soft on Friedl (he's the blonde with the most), Lexi and Rolf spend more than a certain time together. And looking from my balcony the other night, what did I spy but one Baxter escorting Frau Schindler for an evening stroll. All the men (and some of the boys) are losing their eyesight over Erda, the maid. It's that blouse of hers.

One fifth year tried to be funny with her while she was clearing dishes. But Tucker Jenkins shoved his face right into his strudl mit schlag and he's never been the same since.

Jenkins and Humphreys, Cartwright and MacMahon don't seem to do much mountain climbing by day, though there's a lot of ring a ring a roses when the sun goes down. Probably all noise.

The rest of the mob get their jollies annoying the German school across the way. We could have real trouble there.

Patterson clearly has a crush on the little monster with pigtails. He tried to follow her sliding down the banisters yesterday. She remembered the wooden knob sticking up at the bottom and jumped off. He didn't. It was tragic – almost.

More later, Suzanne

Chapter 41

One holidaymaker Suzanne did not include in her letters was Gripper Stebson. Of course she wasn't interested in creatures that crawled out under stones anyway.

But G. Stebson was keeping a low profile on this trip. He did the walking and the touring he was supposed to, spoke when he was spoken to, which wasn't often and generally kept out of the way. It wasn't just that he had observed what happened to the fifth year who tried it on with Erda the maid, and what Jenkins had done to him. Stebson had his dignity and did not intend to end up with a mush full of pie and cream – particularly when there was nothing he could do in return.

No Stebson had other business in mind. He was using his spare time patiently and methodically moving round among the tourists and sizing them up. He talked to some, sussing them out from among the crowds of middle-aged and older tourists who swarmed down into the valleys from Munich to the North. Most of them looked like the old folks at home to him, the blokes balding and beer-bellied, the women dumpy and cardiganned, as though they'd just folded their aprons up and slipped them in a drawer before they came out. They did not – repeat not interest him. He was looking for blokes who had been around in the last lot, who had been with the right mob. Men who had been somewhere, done something, men who carried clout even if they were private these days.

Some he talked to, using the phrases he'd picked up from Rolf. Most of them knew a bit of English. Often though it wasn't enough when it came to talking about the last war. He got the impression though that they were willing to talk about it in general, like old geezers in the boozers at home, but shied off particular questions, like what mob they were in. Some of them gave him some funny looks. One of them let him buy two grosser biers.

Then he backed him up against the cafe wall and sprayed breath over him for nearly two hours while he went on about the Russians. Whether it was what he'd done to the Russians or what they'd done to him, Gripper couldn't make out. But he didn't make that mistake again.

He made another mistake. One lean old man with thinning white hair, and a stern expression stopped him in his tracks.

'You have a bad mind, young man. Der Krieg ist vorbei. War is over. Next time, boom, alles kaput. You should think about good things, schone berge – nice mountains, not Nazi filth.'

What he hadn't bargained for was that he had been noticed. People had talked about him. And someone had their eye on him. They had spotted him before he spotted them. But when they caught his eye he knew – this was it.

One day as he entered the cafe-garden on the edge of the square in Hochwald he became aware of three people at a corner table. Now they were real. An old man, slim, straight-backed, face like a hawk and bronzed, eyes clear, blue and cold, sitting staring in front of him. And a young couple, maybe eighteen or nineteen, young man and woman, like twins, short blonde hair, identical black leather jackets, identical unbuttoned white shirts. The young woman's eye caught his, insolently.

He sat at a nearby table and waited until the old man went silently across the road into a hotel doorway, then he spoke to the young couple. They treated him politely, but with cool contempt. When he offered to buy drinks the young woman seemed about to burst out laughing, but a look from the young man stopped her. In the end they allowed him to buy a round which took almost his last schilling.

'Our grandfather. Oh yes, a war hero definitely, an officer, a dive-bomber pilot.' She *was* laughing at him. But she wasn't lying. She was curious. Every now and then, when she thought Gripper wasn't looking she would exchange glances with her brother. After ten minutes she seemed to become bored. The young man excused himself and they left.

Gripper wandered back up the hill to the farm. He was on to something. But to get more information, he was going to need more money Someone would have to contribute.

Chapter 42

One evening the financial crisis which had been threatening certain members of the party struck Messrs Jones and Maguire.

As a change from football, messing about and annoying the German school over the way (or being annoyed by them) they had gone down into Hochwald to the big cafe on the corner of the square. There you could sit with your coffee and cakes or coke and ice cream and watch the world go by in its braces and shorts and its waistcoat and knickerbockers or its blouses and dirndls, according to your taste. Or if like Messrs Jones and Maguire, you are not interested in that sort of thing, you could simply concentrate on ice cream.

This evening Jonah, studying the menu at their table on the cafe terrace, suddenly noticed something special.

'Look at that,' he pointed at the picture. 'They pour stuff over it and set it on fire. Its called "Heisse Liebe".'

'What's that?'

'Dunno, mate, but who cares.'

'It is called "Hot Love",' said the waitress. 'Are you sure you want it?' She was laughing. That annoyed Jonah.

'Too right we're having it.'

And they did. And it was terrific. The kind of taste that goes to the top of your head and the ends of your toes at the same time. But it was nothing to the buzz they got when the bill came round.

'Forty five schillings?' Jonah felt in his pocket. Then his mouth dropped open. 'That's about £1.30. Crickey. I was thinking about 45p.'

'Well you clown. You didn't expect to get all that for 45p. What are you?'

They emptied their pockets, borrowed from people at

other tables and then crept back up the hill to Schindlerhof, to recover.

Zammo stood by the water trough and kicked the timber sides. 'That's the trouble with just getting 50 rotten schillings a day, isn't it?'

'Don't talk wet. You'd spend the lot in the first three days at that rate.' Jonah stopped and then pointed to the ground under the verandah. 'Do you see what I see?'

'Yes, load of old bottles. What's the use of that. They're all empty and its wine anyway.'

'Listen, numb-top. D'you know how much you get when you take those back to the supermarket?'

'No.'

'Six schillings a throw, that's what. There's about fifteen there. 'Jonah punched his mate on the arm. 'Tomorrow get down here early, with your rucksack. We'll fill up and we'll go down the back way. We don't want anyone else in on this, do we?'

Zammo shook his head.

Next morning early the two slipped out from the farmhouse, loaded up and nipped smartly down the path behind the local church to the supermarket. The way they took brought them out to the rear of the store. Jonah stopped so abruptly that Zammo banged into his back and sent him flying. When Jonah picked himself up though, he was smiling.

'Do you see what I see, Zammo?'

Zammo stared. Behind the back entrance to the supermarket, were stacked piles of metal crates. Each one was filled with empty wine bottles. Cautiously Jonah approached. No one was about. Carefully he selected half a dozen wine bottles, one from each crate and transferred them to his rucksack.

'What's that for?' demanded Zammo.

Jonah smiled: 'Call it re-cycling,' he said.

'Hey, you're crazy,' said Zammo.

'You're chicken, you mean,' retorted Jonah. 'Come on,' he urged.

'Yeah, get on with it,' came another voice.

Jonah and Zammo jumped like the proverbial shot rabbit. Behind them and not more than ten feet away was Gripper. Zammo felt himself heat up inside. He'd let that ape get behind them.

'You can't touch us, Stebson,' he said defiantly.

Gripper smiled, almost pleasantly. 'I'm not going to, but the gaffer in here will. They're very strict over here. Six weeks' breaking stones for what you're doing.'

'Get knotted.'

'No mate. You get in there and get those bottles cashed in. Then come out and give me half. I won't take more, though I should. Little noddies like you ought to be punished. Go on.'

'And,' he added, 'tomorrow, you can do the same. Then we'll all be happy, won't we.'

Chapter 43

While Gripper was up to his little caper, and Jonah and Zammo were up to theirs, someone else was busy.

Next evening, when the Grange Hillites having (some of them) conquered yet another gipfel and got a stamp in their wanderkarte straggled back to the Schindlerhof, tired and weary, they had a little shock.

'Hey, who's been messing about with our gear?' demanded Duane.

Some one had. Every single shoe, sandal and slipper under the verandah bench had been neatly and carefully tied together. It took half an hour to disentangle them and there were some very bad tempered Britishers waiting for their supper at the end of it.

'Three guesses who did it?' said Claire.

'No guesses,' retorted Duane. 'It's the Krauts over the road. Look, when we've noshed, let's go over there and sort 'em out.'

'I heard that,' said Baxter looming over their backs where they sat at table. 'Listen, young man,' he addressed Duane. 'We are here for a holiday, not a military expedition. Apart from which,' he added, 'suppose they sort you out. Some of them look a lot fitter than you people.'

Duane looked as though he were about to protest, but just then in sailed Erda with a huge tray of chicken soup dishes. Half the men in the room immediately leapt up to help. 'Huh,' said Fay, 'isn't it typical. They wouldn't lift a finger otherwise, would they?'

But Annette didn't answer.

'What's up with you then?' demanded Fay.

'Nothing. I was just thinking.'

'Pull the other one. What about? What with?'

'I was thinking there's more ways of killing the cat than choking it with cream.'

'What's that supposed to mean, Old Mother Hubbard?'

'Never you mind,' answered Annette. After supper she approached her old enemies, Jonah and Zammo, and had a quiet word with them. Fay noticed to her annoyance that the three seemed to be in some kind of huddle in the corner of the room.

Next morning the Grange Hillites went on an excursion to Aachensee. As the coaches pulled away down the winding village road, Annette and the others were watching through the open windows.

'Look at that,' she yelled.

Outside the neighbouring farmhouse, a group of German lads had gathered, arguing furiously. As the coaches passed they turned and saluted the British with an assortment of clenched fists and stiff little fingers.

'Hey, what's that for?' asked Claire.

Annette giggled: 'You know that chicken soup last night? Erda was going to throw away the leftovers. She couldn't reheat it. So I made use of it.'

'You did what?' demanded Sutcliffe, suddenly turning in his seat.

'What did you do?' he repeated.

Annette's voice became smaller: 'I shared it out among their boots.'

'That was irresponsible, Annette,' said Sutcliffe, but his voice was drowned in the shout of laughter from the rest of the coach-party.

They got back from their trip in the evening, sunburned (some painfully), refreshed from swimming in ice-cold lake water, sticky from hot sausage and ice cream and generally in good spirits.

Nothing happened that night. The enemy was evidently lying low. The staff made sure no one strayed across the road and there was no sign of the German school. But something was bound to happen.

Chapter 44

Next day, the coaches set out again, down the narrow road through the hamlets and in to the town at the valley bottom and so on to the autobahn leading to the northwest.

'Where we going today?'

'Salzburg. This is the big one. It's about ninety miles or more.'

'But why do we have to go into Germany?'

Rolf smiled at the questions: 'It's the funny way the frontier is shaped, along the river valleys. It makes more sense to cut across a narrow bit of Germany, than run all the way round to stay in Austria.'

'Huh, don't see why the Germans couldn't give you that bit of land and straighten it out.'

'Blimey, mate, the Germans took the whole of Austria in the last lot didn't they?'

'No they didn't. Hitler moved in because the Austrians wanted. Didn't he, Rolf?'

His smile vanished: 'Some did, some didn't. When the time came, it was too late for discussion. Hitler had friends in every country – not only Austria.'

'Yeah, right on. Some English people would have been happy if he'd come over in 1940, my Granddad reckons.'

'Hey what are we stopping for?'

The debate ceased as the coach stopped in a small hamlet half way down the valley. The driver turned:

'I hope you will not mind if three German friends share our coach. We have three spare seats.'

'No,' came the chorus. There were curious stares as the old man murmuring his courteous 'Good morning' and the two young people in their black jackets climbed in. They moved quietly to the back, where people made room for them.

'Hey,' whispered Stew. 'Gripper seems to know them.'

'He would,' answered Duane sourly.

'Wouldn't mind knowing her,' said another lad.

'Down Fido,' answered Claire. 'You're out of your league.'

'What about Gripper? Is he out of his league?'

'Who cares? But she's for the men, not the boys.'

The coach rolled on and from the back seat, the old gentleman who spoke excellent, if slow, English, began to describe the places they were passing, the rivers, hills, castles. He knew their history, anecdotes about the dukes and princes that lived there.

'Countess Maultasch, she was a very ugly woman. They say she was the model for the Duchess in Alice in Wonderland. She gave the Tyrol to Rudolf of Austria.'

Or, 'Salzburg, a marvellous place. Much more than Salt and Mozart,' he chuckled.

Suzanne, who had nipped in smartly to sit next to Rolf, noticed he was not so amused.

'Later, the Tyrol was given to the Bavarian King. It is a lovely place. Many people wanted it.'

'Yes, and Andreas Hofer and the Tyrol rifle brigades won it back,' said Rolf suddenly. There was a silence, which lasted until the frontier had been crossed into Germany.

'Now here,' said the old man, 'the road we are travelling on is the very first motorway in history, the original autobahn.' He paused. 'Built by our Adolf . . .'

There was a slight pause, then McGuffey's voice was heard. 'Yours, not ours.' There was another silence which lasted this time. People talked among themselves until the coaches drew into Salzburg.

Late in the afternoon, dazed with the sun, bewildered with the narrow streets, crowded parks, elegant buildings, stuffed with chocolates and loaded with souvenirs, the Grange Hillites piled into their coaches and pulled out again, heading for Tyrol and Hochwald. Herr Rothkopf played his folk music cassettes pianissimo and soon half the coach-

127

loads were asleep. Then the coach stopped in a small hill town and they were awake again.

'Hey, where's this. We didn't stop here on the way out?'

'What're we stopping for?'

The old gentleman at the rear of the coach was on his feet speaking smoothly.

'I asked Herr Rothkopf and he kindly agreed, to stop a little while here. This is Berchtesgaden, treasured home of our late leader and I was anxious to show my grandchildren. Young people are often ignorant of their own heritage. Perhaps some of our English guests would like to join us.'

'What's all this caper?' came McGuffey's voice. 'We never arranged any tour of Hitler's drawing room.'

'Come on, no need to take it like that,' said Baxter.

'Well, I think it's a liberty,' Sutcliffe spoke sharply.

The old man raised his hand. 'There is no intention to offend. Merely perhaps an interesting aspect of history about which your pupils may not know.'

Rolf was speaking, in German, quietly, but firmly. The old man stiffened, but did not answer. The three left the coach in silence. After twenty minutes, they returned, in silence.

The coaches rolled away and pulled up below the Schindlerhof just as the sun was setting red behind the highest peak.

But the day's excitement was not over.

Chapter 45

That evening after supper, Heidi came running, Pia at her heels, into the farmhouse kitchen. Seconds later she came running out with Rolf, Baxter and McGuffey following her. All rushed across the farmyard followed by those Grange Hillites who were sitting on the verandah steps digesting their speckknodel.

Spread out across the dusty road, and spilling over into the Schindler and Becker farmyards was the father and mother of all dog fights. Only these weren't dogs, they were blokes. No, not all because Annette and some of her mates had become mixed up in it. Around twenty assorted Germans and British were knocking the pimples off each other in no uncertain manner.

It took five minutes shouting, pulling and shoving to break it up, and slightly longer to separate Duane from the German lad whose head he was pounding. Another five minutes was taken to drag the Grange Hill boxing team back into the farmhouse where they were lined up and given a verbal lashing by Baxter.

'What got into your noddy-heads?' he demanded of Duane, whose face showed pretty clearly that he had led the task force into the attack.

'Well they make you sick, the way they ponce about. Think they own the place,' was all Duane would say.

'And they're wrong eh? It's you who owns it?' demanded Baxter.

'They're all the same,' muttered Duane defiantly. 'Look at that geezer on the bus this afternoon. Listening to him you'd think Hitler was still alive.'

Baxter frowned: 'That has nothing to do with it. Hitler was dead more than twenty years before these lads were born. You have been reading too many war comics, my lad.'

'Well, Rolf was choked on the bus today,' retorted Duane, barely remembering, this time, to add 'sir.'

Rolf got up from his seat and came forward into the circle.

'That's true, Duane,' he said quietly. 'I was. Whenever I meet old Nazis like that, it makes the hair crawl on my back.'

'Well, they're all the same. They all thought Hitler was great.'

'Well no, they didn't Duane,' Rolf went on. 'Before Hitler could start his world war, before he and the Nazis began to slaughter the Jews, and millions of other people, they had to kill Germans, and Austrians, who stood in their way.'

'Like . . . ?' Duane began to ask, his voice trailing away.

'Like my grandfather,' said Rolf.

For a moment no one spoke. People shifted around on their seats and where they stood. Baxter cleared his throat.

'I think what we need to do is to go over there, you Duane and the others, and apologize.'

'But, sir,' burst out Annette, 'we didn't start the whole business it's been going on for days now.'

'I know young lady, and you have done your bit, too,' put in Miss Lexington. 'I think we owe it to Frau Schindler to sort things out. We're her guests and fighting on her doorstep is not good enough.'

'Right,' said Baxter. 'Let's sort out who is going.'

Ten minutes later, a dozen Grange Hillites, with staff, plus Rolf and Heidi, were making their way over the farmyard.

'Hey, look,' said Stew.

Across the road, coming in their direction were several of the German lads with their teachers. The two parties stopped and looked at one another. Then Baxter and the leading German teacher both opened their mouths simultaneously and began.

'We would like to . . .'

The whole crowd on both sides of the road burst out laughing.

Chapter 46

While the two schools were having their little reconciliation scene up the hill, Gripper Stebson was at his listening post in the cafe in the Hochwald main square. At this time in the evening it was mainly empty for the night time rush for supper tables with the folk music playing had barely begun.

He was well prepared this time. He had money in his pocket. That very day his two little chimney sweeps, Maguire and Jones had been at work, trading back the supermarket manager's empty bottles to him and had made a generous contribution to the Stebson fund. Now he planned to spend it, wisely.

'Good evening.'

He looked up. The girl in the black leather jacket was at the next table, alone.

'A pity you could not join us, this afternoon?'

Gripper cleared his throat. 'Can I get you . . . ?'

She shook her head: 'When Gerhard, my brother comes, you must be our guest.' She waved a hand at the seat next to her and Stebson quickly sat down. She looked at him.

'You were asking about Grandfather,' she said encouragingly.

'Yeah. I bet he's been places.'

'Oh yes, he has been – places . . .'

Gripper leaned forward. 'Was he in that lot before the war, in Spain, you know, Condor Legion.'

'What's this, Helga?' The brother had arrived and stood behind Gripper's chair. He was tall and the bare forearm that carried his black jacket, was strongly muscled.

'Our friend here was asking if grandfather was with the Condor Legion.' She looked at her brother behind Gripper's shoulder and raised an eyebrow. Gerhard sat down and waved to the waitress.

When the drinks arrived, Gerhard turned to Stebson. His face was hard. Gripper suddenly felt uneasy, a strange feeling for him.

'Why are you asking these questions? When people start asking questions about the past of an old soldier like Grandfather, they usually have a reason. He leads a very private life, now, you understand.'

The way he spoke the word 'private' was chilling. Stebson took a breath. 'It's like this,' he began. Slowly and cautiously he explained to them what he was searching for.

'That's fascinating,' murmured Helga. Stebson could not tell if she were laughing at him. Gerhard frowned at his sister then, after looking carefully at Stebson, he seemed to make a decision.

'Our Grandfather served the Fuehrer from the first until the last. Unlike some others, he did not change his coat when the end came. Because, unlike some others, he does not believe it was the end. In every country leaders like Hitler are required and will be found, not only in Germany, but in England too.' He looked closely at Stebson. 'You understand that?'

For a moment it crossed Gripper's mind that the water here was deeper than he had expected. But he was in now and he wasn't pulling out.

'Yeah. I understand,' he began. But Gerhard seemed not to be listening

'Our Grandfather is one of a select band still living. He was with the Condor Legion. I am surprised you know of it. But you would like a badge from the Legion, a souvenir?'

'No. I've got a use for it,' Gripper was indignant.

'There are very few of them, who have this badge with the great black eagle. When they meet, they call themselves, the Double V, Vogel Verein. You will not understand it, it is what they call a play on words. Something innocent sounding, but . . .'

'Can you get me one?'

132

'That would depend . . .'

'On what?'

'If you deserve it.'

The two suddenly rose and left Gripper sitting alone. There was something chilling about their manner. A warning bell rang in his mind. Was he getting out of his league? The thought made him angry, he didn't scare that easily.

When Stebson got back to the farmhouse, he had a feeling someone had been casing his gear. That could just be Maguire, the little sod, trying to get his money back. Well, he could go on trying.

Chapter 47

Down in the village something was going on. In the meadow by the river an enormous marquee had been put up over night. The air was full of horn and trombone sounds, a lot of them out of tune, and the square filled up in the evenings with men in a fantastic variety of uniform waistcoats, knicker-bockers, stockings and curly brimmed hats with multi-coloured feathers. At the farm, the women brought out embroidered blouses, skirts with masses of stiff frilled white petticoats, magnificent black hats with ribbons.

'What's going on?' demanded Claire of Heidi as she rushed to and fro.

'Corpus Christi,' she answered.

'Who's he when he's at home?'

'It's a special church day. It's not easy to explain, but it's really a big celebration, with bands and dancing and on the last night a tremendous beer festival down in the tent, yodelling, singing, drinking, dancing.'

'Great, can we all come?' demanded Annette.

'Certainly not,' put in Miss Lexington who was just passing, 'we can't have you lot legless, can we?'

'Legless?' asked Heidi. Then she grinned. 'Oh I see, that is very good.' She shook her head. 'You don't have to drink beer. You can have fruit juice and coke and wine. And eat sausages and ice cream and . . .'

'Say, no more, when do we begin . . . ?'

'We begin this afternoon,' announced Baxter, from the door.

'What does that mean?'

'Our friends across the road have challenged us to a two part contest. The first is a football match, to be played before the amazed inhabitants of Hochwald, on the meadow outside the Big Top.'

'What's the second half?'

'That will be revealed after the match.'

That afternoon, Hochwald turned out in force, to say nothing of a mass of tourists game for a laugh. The band of the local fire brigade, splendid in their green and yellow waistcoats, marched round the field, and Mr Rothkopf in his second capacity as Mayor himself turned out to announce the challenge match.

The spectators let out a great roar as the teams took the field, which changed to laughter as they saw the British were fielding four women players.

But they laughed on the other side of their faces when Precious and Annette stormed through the German defences to put the first one in the net.

From then on it was no holds barred. The rumble of the evening earlier in the week, was as nothing to the ferocity of the players now that it was a matter of sport. Rolf as referee had his work cut out. The crowd for their part divided fairly evenly, half rooting for the German side, and half shouting for the Women.

The end came mercifully before the toll of tapped ankles and bruises from brutal shoulder charges brought out the local ambulance team to join the fire brigade. But it was all good clean fun and when the British team marched, or staggered off the field to the tune of *Yellow Submarine* (how the Fire Brigade band knew that, no one could tell), they were leading five three.

It was then that Baxter revealed the second half of the contest. The German school had challenged them to put up a team to cover the three remaining summits on the Hiking Badge card in one day; they marching clockwise, the Grange Hillites marching anti-clockwise.

'Right,' said Baxter, 'we shall want ten volunteers ready with their boots on at 8 o'clock tomorrow morning.'

'I'll come!' shouted Pogo. All stared at him.

'He's mad,' said Stew soothingly.

'Huh, we all are,' said Claire.

Chapter 48

At eight o'clock next morning the two teams had assembled on either side of the village road. The German lads faced up hill, the British downhill. Someone had hastily put together a small piece of cloth with cut-out letters 'G.H.' for the British team. The Germans had a regular pennant with a boar's head. They looked fit and ready for anything. The Grange Hill lot looked fit enough, but didn't all feel it. Pogo, a rosy glow in his cheeks concealing how pale he felt inside, was there, looking nonchalant.

'He's doing it for Heidi, bless him,' said someone.

Pogo looked round murderously. 'Wait till I get back.'

'If you get back.'

'Right,' yelled Baxter. 'Get ready. Remember follow Friedl and don't try to rush ahead. Keep a steady pace, a decent two and a half miles an hour up and down hill should bring you back at four o'clock and make you easy winners. Are we downhearted?'

'No comment,' replied Duane.

There was a sudden bang. The German teachers had a starting pistol (they would) and the two teams were on the road, to the cheers of both sides.

The morning was coolish, a light breeze kept brows from over-heating and the sun was out of sight behind a haze that hung over the slopes. Friedl set a steady pace, and after the first hour as they pushed on uphill towards the first peak, the talking stopped.

At ten o'clock they were there. Friedl halted them and produced his stamp and ink pad: 'Get out your cards,' he called.

'Eh? We haven't time to mess about with cards,' said Pogo.

Friedl shook his head. 'How will anybody know you haven't cheated?'

'What, us? You must be thinking of some other school.'

Hot and thirsty, for the sun had now broken through, they halted on the lower slopes of the second peak to take lunch. Friedl frowned as one or two of the party drained their water bottles.

'Not too much drinking,' he cautioned.

'Ah, we'll sweat it off.'

'No, bad for the stomach,' he warned.

And it was. As they reached the shoulder of the peak, two Grange Hillites were doubled up with cramp. Friedl called a halt for ten minutes.

'Let's shove on,' demanded Duane. 'They can catch up.'

'Don't be stupid,' retorted Claire. 'We've all got to finish.'

At one o'clock the second peak with its obelisk and flagpole was in full view. But so was something else.

'Look,' called Stew, 'just look at that.'

Coming down from the peak, in single file and good order, came the German school. They passed the British in cheerful mood.

'Keep at it. Only fifty more miles to go,' they called.

But there was no reply. The stuffing had been knocked out of some people. The second peak was reached and the cards stamped without a word said.

By three o'clock the pace had slowed to a crawl. Faces were aflame and streaming with sweat, shirts pulled open, and some pulled off, legs were knotting with pain and feet burning as the third and final peak came in sight. Again Friedl halted them.

'Look, you can stop now and rest. The other team has won already. They knew they would. They are hardened walkers, they come here every year. You have done well, believe me.'

'I'm for going on,' said Pogo shortly.

The others stared, but no one argued. The third peak was taken and the party began its limping trek downhill again. Four o'clock had come and gone as they came in sight of the river bridge in Hochwald. Ahead of them, the fire brigade band was playing.

As they hobbled over the bridge and into the meadow, they heard cheers and for the first time saw the newly painted banner over the gate.

'What does that say?' they asked Friedl.

He grinned: 'It says: "Greetings to the English mountain conquerors".'

Chapter 49

When the mountain conquerors got to the marquee after supper it was dusk outside, but inside the huge tent, swaying electric lights on cables made it as light as day. The air was full of the smell of trampled grass and of beer foaming and leaking from massive wooden casks down one side of the canvas hall. At the farther end surrounded by his accordionists, fiddlers and trumpet players who had been playing since crack of dawn and expected to go on all night, the Humorist was telling yet another joke about the peculiar habits of the people in the valley next but one to Hochwald. Every now and then as the music stopped the rumble of conversation was split with the ferocious, 'Hey, hey, hey,' of cheers and counter cheers as dancers from one village after another thumped their way on to the stage.

Tucker Jenkins and his party, Alan, Susi and Pamela, had grabbed a section of one of the long trestle tables near the stage. They were within easy reach of the nearest barrel and the dance floor, and moved from one to the other with greater and greater ease as the evening went by. Pamela was in a jokey mood and seemed to have something up her sleeve. Tucker intended to find out what it was before the end of the evening.

Annette and Fay arrived together. Fay grabbed Rolf for a dance before five minutes had gone by, leaving Annette on her own, but a shout of, 'Over here Miss Keegan', made her turn round to find the lads from the German school at a nearby table. They made room for her, then Claire, and some of the other girls, somewhat to Duane's annoyance. But who should arrive just then, but Pogo, arm in arm with Heidi and half a dozen other girls from Hochwald?

Suddenly Fay squeezed on to the bench at Annette's side.

'Oh, did we get the push, then?' said Annette.

Fay jerked her head to where Rolf was now dancing with Suzanne.

As the music stopped for a moment, Rolf and Suzanne sat down at the corner of a table crowded with members of a visiting band. They had to shout to hear each other.

He grinned: 'Have you enjoyed your time here?'

'Well, believe it or not, I have.'

'I wondered,' he went on, 'you seemed to be on your own so much.'

She shrugged: 'Sometimes I can't stand people. Sometimes I can't stand myself. But don't get the wrong idea. I quite like being on my own and watching what people get up to.'

'Oh?' His eyebrows rose. 'Any particular people?'

'Well, the way people pair off on a holiday like this – the most surprising line ups.'

He laughed: 'You mean like Pogo and Heidi.'

She made a face. 'Since you mention it, no, I was thinking of older people . . .'

'Oo-oh.' He looked sharply at her. 'You haven't been watching the staff, have you?'

'On a holiday like this, you can't help but notice. I mean they let their hair down in the way they can't at school. Shows they're human, I suppose.'

He waited for her to go on.

'Like Miss Mooney. So serious at school. But here the way she's been doing a line on Friedl. Of course, it could be to annoy Sooty Sutcliffe.'

'I see. Anyone else?'

'Since you ask, I have noticed Miss Lexington and yourself now and then.'

He went red. Then he burst out laughing. Now Suzanne went red.

'I'm sorry,' he gasped. 'I don't mean to offend you, but I think you are truly mistaken.'

'Oh, how?' Suzanne was both offended and intrigued.

'Friedl is married. His wife's at university in Vienna. She'll be coming home next week. Friedl is very old-fashioned. Very correct. And so is Miss Mooney.'

'Well, she and Mr Sutcliffe have been off each other.'

He pointed: 'They're dancing together now, and that's the third time.' Then after a pause, he went on: 'I'm sorry, but I'm engaged to be married, Suzanne, and in any case though Miss Lexington is very kind, she is very good to everyone, I think she would find me a little young, and immature.'

'Oh, I wouldn't say that.'

'Thank you. Of course,' he added wickedly, 'you could have included Mr Baxter and Frau Schindler.'

'Oh, not them. They're too steady and o – –'

'You were going to say "old", weren't you. That's the biggest mistake you can make.' He stopped. 'I'm sorry, Suzanne, it's very impertinent of me to lecture you like this. But I didn't want you to get wrong impressions. That would not be fair.'

'Doesn't matter.'

'I hope – you haven't told anyone else what you have observed so far?'

Suzanne shook her head. 'Oh no.'

Oh no! She'd only written three letters with all the sordid details, to Mr Hopwood. Still, she hadn't posted them. She wasn't quite that stupid.

As Rolf went to get drinks, she thought to herself. She'd be going home tomorrow. The time had flown. She'd go and see him in hospital, take some of the chocolate she'd bought, and tell him what had happened, a slightly different version of course.

Chapter 50

The party, at least the Schindlerhof part of it, slowly began to break up. But that was not the end of the action.

Frau Schindler and Friedl took the staff off to the cafe across the square for a final celebration. Before he left, Baxter warned the mountain-conquerors to be back by eleven or face the consequences.

'What are those, sir?' demanded Claire.

'You'll be locked out.'

'Oh, shame, terrible, what'll we do?' came the response.

By and by, though, the others followed, drifting uphill in twos and threes, Grange Hillites arm in arm with Hochwalders and the lads from the German school, laughing, singing, telling jokes.

Only Zammo and Jonah stayed behind. Zammo had caught sight of Stebson through the shifting crowds around the beer barrels. He was with the blonde girl in the black leather jacket.

'I'm going to watch what he gets up to,' he told Jonah.

'You're crazy. You're wasting your time if you reckon you can get that money back now. He's spending it on blondie.'

'I don't think they're going to spend money.'

'Ho, ho.'

'No, don't be funny. I think they're up to something.'

'Ho, ho again.'

'Please yourself. I'm going to keep my eye on him.'

Over at the table near the dance floor, T. Jenkins was having a quiet word with Alan. There wasn't any need to whisper because the noise around was deafening and Pamela and Susi were laughing so hard at something they couldn't have heard anyway. But Tucker was in a conspiratorial mood. He had plans for Ms Cartwright. And he needed a little help from his friends.

'Listen, Alan, when we leave, I'm going on ahead. Now what you do is this. You walk up with Susi and Pam and when you get back by the farmhouse, you make some excuse to take Susi for another walk. That shouldn't be difficult. Take her about five miles up the mountain. The fresh air'll do you both good. The thing is, let Pam go in on her own and give us an hour or two.'

'Oh, yes. And how do we get in?'

'Well, you don't, not in their room. You get in through the window of our room, which I have thoughtfully left open.'

'And what's Susi going to say about that . . .'

'She's your girl, not mine. You're on your own Humphreys. Look, just do it as I say and all will be well.'

'You'll be lucky.'

'They're going,' said Zammo, pointing. Gripper and the blonde girl were moving away towards the entrance to the marquee. 'Come on.'

'I think it's stupid,' said Jonah.

'Look, let's just see where they go.'

Keeping about twenty yards behind, they followed Gripper and the girl along the road, keeping them in sight by the light from the street lamps. Half way up the hill above the meadow, they suddenly turned right into the garden of a small villa, which was in darkness. Watching from the other side of the road, they heard the front door open. A light appeared inside, then vanished.

'Come on,' urged Jonah. 'Let's go back.'

Zammo shook his head. 'No, let's wait just a bit.'

Chapter 51

Tucker, back at the farmhouse, slipped quietly up the stairs to the first landing and in to the room he shared with Alan. Making sure the window on to the balcony was open and could not slam shut if the wind got up, he took off his jacket and slung it on his bed. Next he slipped off his shoes and put on soft-soled sandals. This was commando work, sort of.

Then, he heaved himself up and out through the window on to the balcony. All was quiet here, though over in the old stable building he could hear the kids raising some kind of riot. That wasn't his business.

He paused a second on the balcony and tried the window to Susi and Pamela's room. It was open, but not fastened. That was helpful. He swung the window a little more widely open and then placing both hands on the window sill he vaulted lightly over and in to the room. Move over Romeo.

He landed lightly on an empty bed, stepped down carefully, quietly on to the floor. It creaked. He halted. Now Pamela's bed was over by the door. He aimed himself in the darkness towards it. Then he stopped again. Something was wrong.

He could hear someone breathing. The room wasn't empty. That wasn't right. No they weren't breathing, they were snuffling. Someone was . . .

The bed light suddenly went on. There in Pamela's bed, eiderdown tucked up round her chin, cheeks glowing, eyes alight with mischief, was Erda. She saw the look of amazement in his face, and burst out laughing.

He turned to rush back to the window. But she stopped him.

'If you go, Peter. I shall scream.'

Chapter 52

Gripper knew there was something wrong as soon as he entered the villa from the dark street. As he stood in the unlit hall, the blonde girl close behind him, he realised. She had been alone. Where was her brother? He hesitated. Her hand, lightly, but firmly urged him forward, through an open doorway into an inner room.

As he stood in the centre a light came on. Not a ceiling light, but a shaded wall lamp, red glowing and pointing downwards. From its small light he could see that the windows were heavily curtained.

But underneath the lamp was a portrait. He knew what it was, Hitler in a general's uniform. The portrait was surrounded by black drapes. But beneath it, on a stand, was a red cushion. And in the middle of that was what he was looking for, the badge, heavy in its black, silver and blood red metal, the huge savage bird, wings spread and the words Vogel Verein picked out beneath it.

He moved towards it.

'Wait!' The girl's voice commanded.

The door behind them was closing. Someone else was in the room.

'Do not turn round!'

The door slammed shut.

'Stay where you are. That is the badge you want. But we do not give such things to any one. First you must take an oath to keep secret everything we have told you, everything you have seen and heard.'

Gripper cleared his throat. 'That's easy. I won't.'

'No, you will not. But you will take the oath our way. First our initiation ceremony.'

There was a silence, then she said:

'Take off your clothes.'

145

Chapter 53

Tucker's mouth fell open. Erda laughed out loud. She laughed until the tears came to her eyes. With one hand she pulled the clothes aside. In spite of himself Tucker turned away.

Then Erda jumped on to the floor. She was fully dressed. Tucker knew he'd been set up. He looked at her, grinned, then began to laugh himself. She stepped up close to him and kissed him. Then she put her fingers on her lips. 'Well, you can laugh at yourself. You are a good boy.'

He wasn't so sure if he liked the 'boy' bit.

'I did this, as a favour, for Pamela and Susi. It was a joke. They wanted to, what is it? put you in your place.'

She put her hands on his shoulders. 'Even nice boys get put in their place, now and then.'

He shrugged. The funny side was fading a bit and now he began to feel narked.

She caught his glance, then grinned. 'Now. We play a joke on them, eh?'

'Great, but what?'

'They know I am in here, yes? We lock the door. They think we are in here.'

She crossed to the door and fixed the bolt.

'But we won't be?' He sounded disappointed. She made tut-tutting noises. 'Come,' she said.

She led the way, back through the window, on to the balcony.

Once there she turned to him again.

'Now for a proper joke,' she said and led the way along the balcony, round to the other side of the house. There another bedroom window was open. Signalling for quiet again, Erda slid her leg over the sill and vanished inside.

Tucker hesitated. What did he do now?

Erda's head suddenly appeared in the window again. She beckoned.

'Mach schnell, Peter,' she whispered.

Tucker made quick.

Chapter 54

'Take off your clothes,' commanded the girl again.

Gripper's reflexes went into action.

'You can get . . .' he roared, swinging round, hands up.

But he was too late. The light vanished. He was seized from behind, by neck and elbow. In a flash he remembered the muscular arms of the young man Gerhard. He struggled, lashed out with his foot. A knee caught a nerve centre in his thigh. Pain shot through and the leg went dead, as if paralysed. In that moment his arm was forced up his back and his head was forced down.

Other hands ripped at his jacket, first one arm, then the other. Then his belt. It was for real. They were stripping him and he couldn't do a thing about it. He fought back. But they had hold of neck, arms, legs. There must have been three of them. He remembered the colonel. The old bastard.

They stopped at his shirt. Again the iron hand forced his head down.

'Now, bow to the Leader, bow, you pig, bow.'

As his head and shoulders were forced down and the blood roared behind his eyes, he felt the first blow.

Now Gripper knew the truth. That warning instinct had been right. They were bent. Maniacs – old man, young man, young woman, all three of them. He *was* out of his league.

'Bow, you pig, bow.'

Rage overcame pain and fear. Gripper contorted his body, pulled free, first an arm, then a leg, lashed out with both. Someone grunted. He was free.

Lunging forward in the semidarkness as they stumbled against one another behind him, he reached the wall. There was another door.

He snatched it open, crashed down a passage, through

another doorway, out across a small yard, over a low fence and down a grass bank.

He was dressed only in his shirt, but he did not stop to think about it. He was getting out of this.

Chapter 55

After ten minutes waiting in the dark outside the villa, Jonah said, 'Look, mate. If you're not going, I am. Come on. He's going to be there all night. You've had it.'

Reluctantly Zammo was persuaded and they set off up the hill road towards the farm.

They were about half way up the slope when they heard the car behind them.

'Hey, they're flogging that, aren't they?' said Jonah. Headlights suddenly filled the narrow road and the car engine seemed on top of them.

'Must be half cut. Hey look out mate.'

Jonah shoved Zammo off the road and leapt aside himself as the car tore past. As he picked himself up from the grass, he felt something strike his head, something soft, like cloth. Snatching at it he held it out in front of him just as Zammo regained his feet.

'Look at that. It's a pair of jeans. How crazy can you get?'

'Come here,' said Zammo. He took the jeans from Jonah's hand and carried them across to the nearest road lamp.

'Look at that, mate,' he said, 'that belt, that buckle. Do you recognise that gear?'

Jonah stared. 'That's Stebson's.' Then he grabbed Zammo's arm. 'I've got an idea, what we can do with these.' He started off again at a run up the hill towards the Schindlerhoff, Zammo close behind him.

When they reached the verandah, they stopped. The outer door was locked.

'Hey, Zammo, we're locked out. I told you we shouldn't have hung about.'

'Well, hang about now,' said Zammo, sitting down on the steps with the jeans over his knees. 'Here's the good news.

He's got a pocket on his belt, and, if I'm not mistaken, it's got money in it – our money.'

They were sharing the money between them when they heard quiet footsteps and low voices in the yard. Quick as a flash, Zammo hid the jeans under the verandah. But he was not quick enough with the money. Standing there looking down at them were Frau Schindler and Baxter.

'Well, now,' said Baxter. 'There must be a story behind that. Hadn't you better tell me?' His voice was friendly, but there was an edge to it that they recognised all too well.

Slowly and reluctantly, Jonah explained the history of the bottles, the deposit money, and Gripper's extortion racket.

'We were only taking back our lot,' he said.

'You mean the supermarket's lot,' said Baxter. He looked down on them. 'What must Frau Schindler think about us?'

Frau Schindler shook her head. 'I would be more angry – if it were not a trick some of our boys play.' She looked at them. 'If you will let me have what does not belong to you, I will see that it goes back where it belongs, perhaps after you have gone home.'

'Well, that's more than you two deserve,' said Baxter. 'Now inside, and straight to bed.'

Chapter 56

Gripper's ordeal was not yet over.

Tying his shirt tails between his legs, disregarding the pain which ran in waves from shoulder to calves, he ran quickly, crouching low, back on to the road and up the hill. As he came round the corner of the villa he heard the car start and roar away in front of him. Bastards, he thought, and the thought brought the water back to his eyes.

As he came up to the farmyard, he heard voices. He stopped. There were people on the verandah. Shifting from one leg to another he waited. At last the talking ceased. He heard the door close and stealthily came forward and up on to the verandah.

The door was locked again. He came within an ace of kicking it in his fury, but remembered in time, his feet were bare.

Back to the yard he went and circled the house. At the side he discovered a balcony with an open window. It looked like a window on to a landing. He wasted no more time, but clambered up over the rail. In ten seconds flat, he was in through the narrow opening and dropping down inside the window.

There was a sudden commotion. Someone yelled at him. For the second time that evening, rough hands seized him. He was dragged to a door and thrust out into the passage. Almost beside himself with pain and rage, he crawled into the dormitory. Here he was in luck. All was quiet and in darkness. He clambered into his bunk and slowly, uncomfortably, he went to sleep.

One thing had kept him going through the whole sorry caper. As he had fought his way from the room and escaped through the villa back door, his quick fingers had seized the badge from its mounting. He still had it clutched in his fingers. He felt its hard edge as he drifted away.

Next morning as he went down to breakfast he saw people grinning and looking sideways. What did they know? Baffled he went outside on the verandah where a group of second years was laughing and pointing. From the flagpole dangled his jeans.

And a handwritten notice said: '2000 miles – only one owner.'

Last Words

They all got home safely, bronzed and fit. Pogo Patterson weighed himself on a machine at the airport, discovered he was six pounds lighter and went round with his sponsor sheet trying to collect money from people who had promised it. He got about sixty five groschen (2p).

Annette and Fay came back with addresses for about two million pen friends, promising faithfully to write to everyone.

When Suzanne got home, she read through her letters to Mr Hopwood, had a few laughs, including one at herself, and tore the letters up. Couldn't have Mr Hopwood seeing them – or anyone else, for that matter. Especially not after that business with Claire Scott last year.

Duane and Claire seemed to have made it up. Though Duane still hasn't admitted he told the local rag about the ladies' football team. It is anybody's guess what Claire will do if she finds out.

Miss Mooney and Graham Sutcliffe seemed to have made it up. It must have been something in the air or the water up there, but they came back in a good mood. Baxter, they say, is planning a winter holiday, without skis.

Tucker Jenkins felt he had done all right in the end. As far as Cartwright was concerned, the score was a draw, but there wouldn't be a replay.

Jonah stayed the rest of the holiday with his Aunt and he and Zammo messed about to their hearts' content. They kept clear of money-raising schemes, though. They kept a close watch out for Gripper but he seemed to have gone to earth.

What happened to Gripper was this. A few days after he got back home, he could not resist going round to the old man's flat to show him his Condor Legion badge.

The old bloke took one look at it and laughed in his face.

'You've been done, mate. D'you know what that means – Vogel Verein? It means Bird Club – bleeding bird watchers.'

Gripper started to tell the old man what he thought of him, but the door was slammed in his face. As he turned angrily to go he saw an old woman with a shopping bag watching him.

'You want to keep clear of that one, son. He's bent,' she said.

Gripper shrugged: 'Well, I expect it was the war that did it,' he answered.

She laughed; 'Get off with you. The nearest he came to the war, was watching John Mills shooting Jerries down at the pictures. What's he been telling you?'

Gripper didn't answer. He turned his back and sloped off down the stairs.

Daredevils or Scaredycats
Chris Powling

'Thanks for saving my place, Mush. I'll have it now.'

Fatty Rosewell was a big bully. Every Saturday he used threats and fists to get himself one of the best places in the cinema queue. When Fatty picked on David Clifford, he was looking his most weed-like, all glasses and hair, but weedy David gave all the kids in the queue, not least Fatty Rosewell, a big surprise that morning.

Sometimes it's hard to know where cowardice ends and bravery begins. The most unlikely scaredycats can suddenly turn into heroes. In the course of their adventures, Teddy, Kit, Pete and Jimmy begin to find out just how many different kinds of courage there are.

'Entertaining and realistic, the stories take us into a world of dare and counter-dare, bluff and counter-bluff, catcall and playground scuffle.'

Recent Children's Fiction

The Fib and other stories

GEORGE LAYTON

I was sick of Gordon Barraclough: sick of his bullying and his
shouting, and his crawling round Mr Melrose, sick of him being
a good footballer and going on about my old football gear. So I
told him it had belonged to my uncle, who'd scored thousands
of goals – because my uncle was Bobby Charlton! That was the
fib. Then Bobby Charlton turned up as the surprise celebrity to
switch on the Christmas lights outside the town hall. 'You're in
for it now,' said Gordon, 'I told him you said he's your uncle.' I
looked up at Bobby Charlton. He looked down at me. If only the
earth would open and swallow me up . . .

Based on George Layton's own childhood, here are ten short,
funny stories that come straight to the point on many important
issues of adolescent life, such as school, girlfriends, football,
and the problems of keeping in with your mates and getting
round mum.

Albeson and the Germans

JAN NEEDLE

It seems a very simple thing that starts off all the trouble – a rumour that two German children are coming to Church Street School. Although the teachers cannot understand the panic that this causes, Albeson can. His comics, and his dead grandfather have taught him all about Germans. And he doesn't fancy the idea one little bit.

The plan that Albeson's friend Pam comes up with frightens him stiff. Unfortunately, his mate Smithie, who's very tough and sometimes a bit odd, likes the idea. So Albeson has no choice. From then on, everything Albeson does gets him deeper and deeper into trouble, and finally, danger.

'Gripping, lively and funny – It really grabs you'

Daily Mirror

My Mate Shofiq
JAN NEEDLE

Since his best friend got himself killed playing chicken on the railway line, Bernard Kershaw has been at a loose end. He's got a gang, including a dead-smart girl called Maureen, but they don't do the sort of exciting things they used to.

His life at home's a mess as well, because his mum is ill in a way he doesn't like to think about. Although he still dreams about being a secret agent, or winning the war single-handed, things aren't really all that good.

Then one morning he sees the quiet Pakistani boy in his class turn into a violent fury to sort out a gang who are stoning some little 'curry kids'. Bernard gets involved, without meaning to at all, and finds himself up against the toughest bullies in the school.

He also finds himself in trouble of a different kind. For Shofiq's family, too, are in a bad way, and the grown-up people who are trying to help them appear to the boys to be set on breaking up everything.

Their attempts to stave off these disasters, and to make some sense of the things they see happening all around them, lead Bernard and Shofiq into confusion and violence.

'It's an angry and powerful novel – but much of it is very funny. The characterization is excellent; the dialogue is vivid. Thoroughly recommended.' *Reviewsheet*

Harold and Bella, Jammy and Me

ROBERT LEESON

Our gang, Harold and Bella, Jammy and me, was always getting into some scrape or other: Playing Hallowe'en tricks on the Tunnel Top gang . . . Coming home soaked after we'd found the bridge over the stream up in the woods, and the other lot happened to come along . . . Investigating the caves where we'd heard King Arthur and his knights still slept . . .

Brimful of colourful characters and adventures, this is a lively and funny collection of stories about a group of children growing up in a Northern town.

Also in Lions by Robert Leeson are *Challenge in the Dark, The Demon Bike Rider, The Third Class Genie, Grange Hill Rules, O.K?, Grange Hill Goes Wild, Grange Hill For Sale* and *It's My Life.*